MW00603952

MOSAIC

WHO PAID FOR THE BULLET?

a novel of the Civil Rights Era by

Michael Meltsner

QUID PRO BOOKS

New Orleans, Louisiana

Copyright © 2022 by Michael Meltsner. All rights reserved. No part of this book may be reproduced by any mechanical, photographic, or electronic process, or other recording, nor may it be stored in a retrieval system, transmitted, or otherwise copied for public or private use—other than for "fair use"—without the written permission of the publisher.

Published in 2022 by Quid Pro Books.

ISBN 978-1-61027-452-4 (pbk.)
ISBN 978-1-61027-453-1 (hbk.)
ISBN 978-1-61027-455-5 (ePUB)
ISBN 978-1-61027-454-8 (trade pbk.)

QUID PRO BOOKS
Quid Pro, LLC
5860 Citrus Blvd., suite D
New Orleans, Louisiana 70123
www.quidprobooks.com

qp

Publisher's Cataloging-in-Publication

Meltsner, Michael.
    Mosaic : who paid for the bullet? / Michael Meltsner
        p. cm.
    ISBN 978-1-61027-452-4 (paperback, mass mkt.)

1. Murder—Fiction. 2. Twentieth Century—Fiction. 3. Alabama—Fiction. I. Title.

PS 3601 .D356 M17 2022   2022156231

This is a work of fiction. All characters, places and incidents are used fictitiously, and any resemblance to any person, living or dead, or to any place or incident, is entirely coincidental.

MOSAIC

For Margaret Burnham and David Barton Smith

and in memory of Jim Nabrit and John L. LeFlore

Other Books by Michael Meltsner

WITH PASSION:
AN ACTIVIST LAWYER'S LIFE

IN OUR NAME:
A PLAY OF THE TORTURE YEARS

RAPE, RACE AND JUSTICE (EDITOR AND PREFACE)

THE MAKING OF A CIVIL RIGHTS LAWYER

REFLECTIONS ON CLINICAL LEGAL EDUCATION
(WITH P. SCHRAG)

SHORT TAKES: A NOVEL

TOWARD SIMULATION IN LEGAL EDUCATION:
AN EXPERIMENTAL COURSE IN PRETRIAL LITIGATION
(WITH P. SCHRAG)

PUBLIC INTEREST ADVOCACY:
MATERIALS FOR CLINICAL LEGAL EDUCATION
(WITH P. SCHRAG)

CRUEL AND UNUSUAL:
THE SUPREME COURT AND CAPITAL PUNISHMENT

MOSAIC

"The important thing to know about an assassination
or an attempted assassination is not who fired the shot,
but who paid for the bullet."

Eric Ambler, *A Coffin for Dimitrios*

"I will remember that I remain a member of society, with special
obligations to all my fellow human beings, those sound of mind
and body as well as the infirm."

From a modern version of the Hippocratic Oath

"...think not of revenging yourself upon this caitiff."

William Harrison Ainsworth

North

When you are in love, truly in love, the boundary slips. Two selves merge. Injury to her was injury me. The injury was murder, the redress had to be punishment that fit the crime. What surprised me. What I suddenly knew—I'd never be free of it. The pleasure of revenge would not be followed by catharsis. Lawyers of my sort know ambivalence to the bone. We talk either/or, Black and white, guilty or innocent ... but in fact know gray is the color by which life turns. But, one way or another, it would have to get done. I owed it to her. No that's not really it. I owe it to the memory of her I have to live with for the rest of my life.

It's in my hands. And I'm not going to share responsibility with the government. Leave the law to the side; do it myself. But make sure who and how. This is all that is left of my sense of justice.

McSorely 1966

Sometimes you have a thought that disgusts you. *A body built for sex.* So you push it away. Hard to get rid of, catching his breath at her beauty. A perfect corpse just lying there.

McSorely was the wrong cop to get the call. No, he didn't mean it should have gone to another officer. It was his responsibility; he was the boss, the chief of detectives. He grew up in Jersey City, New Jersey, a place where you don't necessarily ever go to Manhattan but you can always see it, never forget the Big Apple is there. Back when he was a kid, his town was known as the most corrupt in the country. He still didn't know how he'd ended up here in Gulf City. Much less how he'd spent most of his life in the real South, listening to his supposed colleagues and pals make fun of his accent.

His father was the kind of heavy drinker, loud talker who gives the Irish a bad name. He moved the family to South Florida, which is definitely not the real South, when McSorely was ten. He told them it was for a better job but the only work they ever saw him do was regularly arranging, with a fat man who always had a cigar stuck in a corner of his mouth, to move cartons of cigarettes and boxes labeled Johnny Walker Black Label from a van to and from their garage. This happened a lot; the bottles would always be gone in a week. Aside from this, he kept what he was doing to himself. Money was always short in the family. McSorely had four brothers and a sister and his father was around the house during the day all the time, not doing much of anything so far as they could see. Maybe that's one of the reasons McSorely got out early and moved here.

Before she died, his mother got a little looney and talked about how they were owed something by the Miami mob, only she never used the word "mob." She would call them "the shadows" but she meant the mob. His father was long gone by then and couldn't be asked. McSorely knew this wasn't a background that signaled a career in law enforcement, but here he was. Having a desk job, to put it kindly, meant being overweight. He didn't exercise enough and his wife favored food fried. She was as Southern as they come when it had to do with cooking.

The call came in early. McSorely was having his coffee from the take-out place, which he liked strong and black. The desk officer was in the john so he took it. Should have let it ring. This was before there was anything like 911. It came from an old man who was freaking out. He found his stepdaughter lying on the porch. "Do something. Do something," he shouted into the phone. McSorely finally got an address from him so he knew right away they were white. He ordered an ambulance. With a street patrol guy he sometimes worked with, one of the few locals he really trusted—officer Perkins—he got out there and found her.

Right away he didn't like it. A dead youngish white woman, lying facedown on a small front porch. Wearing a long cream-colored nightgown. The hem was pushed up well over her knees. He put his hand over his eyes to seal off his first thought. But then he had to become his professional self. Might there be a sexual assault involved? Of course, that never checked out. Without moving her you could see congealed blood under her front so she'd been shot hours before. Was that a bruise he saw on the side of her neck? He should have spent more time studying it.

Down on his knees, Perkins took a look, a strange expression on his face. He told McSorely there was a revolver under her body. They talked to the stepfather. His wife, her mother, was in a nursing home recovering from surgery. He kept repeating things the police obviously knew. He was really a whimpering mess. Hadn't heard anything. You could see the wires of his hearing aid sticking out of his ears. He kept saying something that at the time was odd: "But she's a doctor. But she's a doctor." As if doctors couldn't be shot.

But then McSorely looked closer and finally figured out who she was. He knew right then they had trouble. He didn't want to know.

When they looked inside, there was a table in the front room with a pile of papers and a small tortoise shell reading lamp. The light was turned on. Apparently, she'd been writing a letter. Probably around bedtime. Or maybe she just couldn't sleep. It was to someone she called "Dear one." It began, "We should talk soon." And that was it. Interrupted then, McSorely surmised. The table was near a cracked window glass. He'd say about four inches in length. Later, on the grass near the window, Perkins found a stone. The stepfather thought that the Browning 9mm was hers but he wasn't sure. McSorely wanted to get the coroner involved soon.

McSorely thought, *everybody knows this is a gun friendly area and we have our share of homicides—but few look like this. White woman. Stable neighborhood. Her own home. Except for the window, no sign of burglary.* But knowing who she was in this town, he wasn't surprised. A chief of detectives hears things and she was a different type of person in a city not in love with difference.

An hour after McSorely got back to the station, there was the call. It wasn't a surprise.

The last time the director at Davis Memorial, Hedley Ronson, called him it was about a young doctor—the son of the chief of dermatology at his hospital—who had been suspected of trying to end the pregnancy of a nurse he'd been poking nightly in a closet where staff stored linen and gowns. The girl had died. He was calling, Ronson said, as a courtesy. He'd already talked to the City prosecutor; they agreed that while the botched operation was probably the cause of death, the evidence of evil intent or reckless behavior was too thin to prove beyond a reasonable doubt. And why, in that case, Ronson asked, end the promising career of the young doctor because the police were taking a different view? He just wanted McSorely to know the way he saw things.

Maybe the father of this young doc was too busy to call himself now that he had a bigtime reputation for inventing a new way of getting rid of skin cancer. Or maybe he was just too highfaluting. But, more likely, he knew that when Hedley Ronson got involved McSorely would be hearing from the part of the City that decided most things. A journalist had given the group of movers and shakers a pithy name but he could never remember what the man called it, probably because he really liked to say his own moniker for them— The Posse! In the end, the DA found a way to turn the young doctor's behavior over to a medical review board. Criminal charges were never lodged.

This call was pretty much the same sort of thing. Ronson laid it out straightaway: So sad what had happened. The dead woman was such a promising colleague. First in her class at med school. A great career ahead of her. She had a gift for diagnosis and it didn't hurt she was quite a beauty, though to tell the God-honest truth he preferred the way she looked before she cut her hair. "But Mac let me confide," he said, suddenly lowering his voice, "there was a trust issue."

"What the hell," McSorely asked him, "did you mean by that?"

He laughed and went on. Not a guy who answers questions unless he wants to. "There are simply other matters involved," he said.

There was a case they all knew about where old doc Foster Hawkins had sent a teenage patient home with aspirin and an Rx for bedrest when it was really appendicitis. Somehow, Doctor Clem got involved and caught it in time. Got the kid into surgery. Not sure how she even knew to intervene.

McSorely just let him talk on but finally Ronson got to the point: Because Clem was the town maverick—"you know she let colored patients sit in the same waiting room of her private office with her white patients and she made sure everyone knew about it"—the race mixers were going to grab onto this and make it into a big issue. Davis Memorial had an application pending for major government financing of a new wing that was going to put the hospital and Gulf City on the medical map. It would include very powerful and expensive scanners, a hyperbaric chamber to fight burns, and the rest of what was required to bring patients from all over the country to their doorstep. He threw out the kind of doc-speak jargon words like "hypoxia" that are supposed to shut you up. And, he added, it meant jobs.

Then Ronson's voice raised close to a shout; he was emotional all right: "They were out there, the integration police—no offense but that's what we call them—and they're actually trying to force our physicians to place patients in particular rooms even if it would cause them deep anxiety and disturbance. Can you imagine? Now while we are a non-discriminatory institution," he added calming down a bit, "I made sure the U.S. Surgeon General himself knew in no uncertain terms that it is up to our doctors to decide a patient's room and who takes care of them."

He went on: "I'm sure you agree we need to keep the present matter sensible. I won't let this unpleasantness stand in the way of institutional growth. Please understand that it was most certainly an accident. Poor woman must have been frightened by night birds or Mardi Gras types rehearsing or even some white-trash or nigra burglars. She must have taken prudent steps to defend herself by getting a weapon and, you know, just tripped. The gun fired. How regrettable. Women just don't know how to deal with firearms."

"Thanks for your call, Doctor," McSorely told him. "I mean thanks Director. We'll treat this in the regular way, the way it deserves." McSorely made sure he sounded cooperative; had to be careful here because to tell the truth he had a grudge against this guy. He was the surgeon who told McSorely's wife that tests revealed she had to lose both breasts because of a genetic cancer risk. He didn't do the surgery but he was the referring physician and they went along but it was the wrong thing to do. She never really recovered a feeling of goodness after she learned that what they found wasn't as bad as Ronson told her. But she was a brave one. More than McSorely. While she didn't let her feelings out, he still knew she wasn't the same. Of course, he said nothing about this to Ronson. He was used to putting it aside.

"We'll be looking for that report," he said.

"Yes," McSorely said, again making sure he was Officer Agreeable, and he added that Ronson had a point there with the female of the species. They weren't made to handle guns, and then McSorely added, just out of a desire to turn the screw a little bit because he didn't like these Posse powerplays, "Oh yes, you are so right about the weaker sex, but remember Doctor Clem was in the War. Somewhere near the frontlines in Italy. She might know something about guns—though more likely she was just a typist."

Of course, Ronson ignored that and concluded by saying he was sure the coroner was going to officially declare her death accidental—a prediction that at that early point troubled McSorely, if it was true. It came to him that he didn't believe there was any accident. Ronson's call made him more certain even though there was no proof to the contrary. Just a cop's instinct, the kind of feeling that would get him nothing but grief if voiced, much less if he acted upon it. He hadn't gotten to be chief of detectives by being stupid. If it was declared a homicide, the way Gulf City law works, the rest of the Department as well as the prosecutor would assume the killer was an African American burglar who managed to get at her gun while she was resisting. He probably had a car waiting and picked her house randomly. They might actually go out and find some buck with a criminal record to take the fall. It had been done before in case you don't know.

One of the reasons McSorely was such an oddity here was that his first thought would have been one of the ragtag, often drunk, ignorant, angry white men who this town was full of. These guys often had a Klan connection even if they didn't go to meetings. McSorely was kind of ashamed at the thought because you could imagine overhearing a conversation between Posse members, suggesting they search for such a resentful white male who probably worked at a job that got his hands greasy; one who had a record of treating women badly. This was, of course, the profile of the trash types he had seen in the Klaverns. That was during his more active days; now he was a desk jockey with too much weight and a bit of the arthritis in his right hip. Back then, he wasn't interested in the Rotarians, the Lions, Elks or even the American Legion. But the Sheets had all the attributes of a lodge like those, with the exception that they produced a long list of racial crimes from cussing young people to cheating sharecroppers to house and barn burning to beatings—at times random but more often targeting an out-of-place move by a Black male—to the ultimate crime of lynching, always done in concert, never alone.

But it didn't fit here. The doctor wouldn't come up on the Klan enemy list; she was a local female, not some intruder from New York. She had a reputation all right, but she was a rebel against her own people, the people at the top. And while most of the thinking on this murky subject in this town skirted reasonable inquiries into things like evidence, she was also known for not charging patients who couldn't pay.

McSorely thought that if a mind reader really knew him—and for God's sake it was good that no one fit the bill—he would see that for most of his career, he had been a typical beat cop of the South, coming down hard on anything that looked like disrespectful or challenging behavior from the colored population, even when it was more provocative than criminal. But his attitude had altered, became more evidence-based you might say, once he made detective and now as chief, of course. He realized he had to look at the world in a different way. To be honest, the dream that haunted him some nights was of a mob coming to a jail, his jail or one that looked like the one he knew best, demanding the "colored rapist." He stood in a doorway in this dream with his service revolver drawn, telling the men at the front that he will surely die but certainly some of them will too if they don't desist. The dream is like a movie he'd seen or maybe just imagined. Only on awakening, McSorely was never sure he'd have the courage. They might strip him of my firearm easily and beat him badly. Or worse. But, hell, would he even try to stop them? Would he have had the guts? They say this sort of thing no longer happens. But it does. Not only in his dreams. And his dreams, they end too soon; he never finds out if he has the courage.

North 1964

Awake, North's first thought made him close his eyes—as if it would help him forget. Today would be the day he told his son; then the change would be sealed. A whining noise shivering through the old house distracted him. At first, he thought it was Graft, but as his eyes took in the blade of gray New England dawn slanting across a broken blind he knew the whining for what it was, could only be. Not the moaning of his cowardly German shepherd, an animal no longer able even to frighten away a first offender. Not the wind. But Wynne. His son getting in a last one before crew practice.

North turned on his stomach and pulled the quilt over his head, trying to forget what he had decided, had to tell. This would be the day he would say goodbye to his Depression Baby fear of the unknown. But like the trial lawyer he was, the next thought was adversarial. *I'm just going along with the new times.* Beatniks, Sit-ins, Peyote, Rock is taking us somewhere but he couldn't really name where it was. He felt unleashed. At least he would no longer just be a conduit to prison.

I'd better oil that kid's bed, he thought, *before he sends the springs to the floor, before I strangle him.* Lying there as thoughts

9

crowded in, he could usually distract himself. But unlike his son, North was simply not good at pressing satisfaction from his own body. Too lean and tall and dry. He turned to a foolish tapestry of revenge: getting back at the mechanic he'd dealt with the day before at Sonic Boom Audio in Concord where he had been charged forty-five bucks to fix a radio that didn't need fixing. The whole thing, trivial as it was, offended his sense of right. Perhaps, he should suggest to the IRS that there was some skimming going on at retail stores near the historic "Rude bridge that arched the flood." That would not, of course, be very Thoreau-like in spirit. Was he losing his grip? Instead of telling the mechanic it was just too much money, he'd banged on the counter with his fist and looked hard, profoundly hard. He hadn't said anything, probably because he really knew he was in the wrong. He thought that the machine was defective. The mechanic had to be paid for his time whether or not it was. North recognized his grievances had nothing to do with the loss of a few dollars but the thoughts came anyway.

Transitions are hell, he told himself. Instead of shrugging the episode off, Diana would have said if she was still around, "You had to give them the prosecutorial stare. Couldn't let it go. The look that says you've been crossed. What, no words, Chris? Graft got your tongue?"

And she was right, which was just one reason of many why he had to make a change. Strangely, he was confident that the change he had in mind would work because he recognized that he was fed up with himself. The self he had fallen into, he proposed when he needed consolation, was an adulthood that simply copied what it had known before. This was best rationalization he could come up with but he also believed it was on him that he wasn't on the right path. *Face it, I made a choice even if I didn't think of it that way. What you do is what you choose.*

When Diana and Christopher North argued, Wynne merely watched. If he took sides, he did so silently. North thought his son had learned the virtues of tactful withdrawal from years of shuttling between his mother and father and had then applied the lesson to his father and stepmother when his father remarried. The silence increased the barrier between the father and son because of the implied judgment. Was his son just accumulating evidence he might use to eventually decide his primary allegiance? Or maybe he was getting ready to declare he was a grownup who didn't need either of them. North had once come upon the boy hanging out with a group of his high school friends in Cambridge, in Harvard Square near the subway entrance. The kids were all smoking. Wynne was waving his cigarette like a baton, talking quickly, gesturing excitedly. Though nothing much seemed to be happening, he was involved. North had smiled as he passed by, unseen at first, and casually patted Wynne's shoulder before continuing with his errands, but he had been shocked by the experience. How little he knew of his son. Someone with a character of his own, a self he never betrayed to his father.

Recently, Wynne had moved from what North had hoped was a wise neutrality to a kind of exploitative indifference. His father had a bed for him in the large creaky house where the shifting population of graduate students helped pay the carrying charges on the mortgage. Wynne used it. His mother, Susan, North's first wife, was always ready to cook him a double-sized meal in her Newton apartment. Wynne would be there. Harvard had a room for him that was only two blocks from the rowing shed. All right, sometimes Wynne would sleep there. What did you ask such a kid? What was he studying? North wondered what that would produce. He would give it a try.

Wynne spent four hours a day sculling on the Charles. In the winter, he grunted in the blocks at the drafty red-shingled Victorian boathouse, groaning his body love in the crimson sweatsuit he hated to take off. Sore legs, running nose, and neck like a block of wood, calves you couldn't get your hands around. Even splinters in the ass. Nothing kept the kid from stroking. From what North could tell, Wynne's Harvard education involved crew and girls. He might also sit in large-ish lecture halls taking notes—but if so North never heard about it. Maybe Susan got the classroom reports while it was the girls Wynne showed his father. The son had tri-vided his life and the father got to see the girls because the boy had decided that it was appropriate to bring them to the yellow house in Concord. Wynne really had three homes—one in a Harvard dorm with an old New England surname, one at his mother's apartment, and one in Ye Olde Concord. Had his son carved a zone in each? Did he study at his mother's and take crew on the Charles River with the same intensity he used the springs in the room on the second floor that had been North's study before his separation from his second wife had required some changes in the layout of the yellow house?

North felt blindly for his sneakers, pulled on the blue terrycloth robe that needed laundering, and padded through the kitchen to let Graft out in the backyard. He stepped into the mud room and opened the door to a typical New England drizzly day, a faint taste of salt in the air. He nudged the old dog with his foot, while staring blankly at the puddles forming on the granite stepping stones.

"Dad." The boy was in the kitchen. "One minute," North mumbled.

"Dad."

North turned away. "Hold on I have to pee." North couldn't face the day without some hot water on his face. He heard a lot of noise, muffled through the familiar morning sound of plumbing; another intrusion to avoid as he opened the door to the downstairs bathroom. Had a finger in his ear to pull out some crud.

"Occupado. Hey."

"What! Oh, sorry, sorry, didn't know." Sliding in between him and the flash of color, the girl and her panties at the mirror, Wynne look exasperated as North finally fully opened his eyes.

"Dad, I told you that Sylvie was in the john."

"Ok, ok," North retreated. His mouth open, his head shaking. "Didn't hear. Sorry son."

Later, over coffee, camp coffee, North asked his flesh and blood, only begotten son, taller than him by a fistful of inches, weighing in at about 195, what he was studying these days. During college North had spent one summer as an apprentice ranger in the Teton Mountains. His boss, Samie Redpath, had made his coffee by cooking water with the grounds. After Diana left, North reverted to Samie's way of brewing. He allowed himself to strain out the grounds. The girl watched this procedure as if Wynne's father was a true eccentric. She had an exquisite chest, and wore a robin-egg-blue turtleneck neatly tucked into her jeans, reminding North of dark thoughts a father should never have in the presence of a son's woman.

"So, tell me what are you studying these days?"

Wynne's response was silence, then a look that could be read as saying *knock it off*. But then hurried words in deference to paternity. "Not much. The usual." The boy stared into his bowl of cereal. He could have been eight years old. Sylvie tittered.

"But I really want to know. I'm paying the bills, I should have a quarterly report."

"Twenty percent."

"What?"

"Remember I'm on loans. The University comes up with eighty

percent; you're paying twenty. You're only a minority shareholder."

Bingo, thought North. *The kid is quick.* "Well, ok, give me at least a one fifth of a report."

"I've got a paper due on Structuralism."

"Of course, Structuralism."

"Yeah, Claude Lévi-Strauss and the structuralists."

"Sure."

"With special emphasis on ritual. Also, linguistic models, semiotics. Information theory, you know."

"What else?"

"I've an exam in nuts and sluts. Pass the muffins... Please."

"What's that?"

"Abnormal psych. And the jam. Dad, have you been watching too much television lately?" North ignored him.

North turned to the girl. "And you, young lady, do you go to school?" *How wooden I sound*, North thought. *Young lady indeed. Why so stiff and parental?* Scourge of crooks and con artists, he knew when he was beaten. Over age thirty, North had previously decided many things. One was not to worry when life made you a straight man. *Play that part well, with grace.* The trick was to do it and watch. Participate as well as observe. Occasionally try to throw in a twist of wit even though it would rarely be caught. Yes, he did have to make a change in the way he lived or he would grow old before his time.

Sylvie and Wynne exchanged a glance. *Am I being hostile again?* the father wondered. *It would be grossly unfair to charge me with insensitivity to women*, he thought. *I just hold them to the same standards. Anyhow, it isn't women. Was it Diana? Was it Susan?* No, no he would be making a change because he had to admit it was him.

"Unisex Massage."

The toast popped in the silence. Father and son rose, chairs scraping. Then paused. Feint, dip, laugh. At last, the laughter. The best way he connected with his son when Wynne was younger was to make him understand there was an elephant in the trunk of the family car or that he was having lunch that day with the front four of the New York Giants or he was about to prosecute Elvis on a major drug change: "Yes, son, caught him with a guitar case full of snow. You wouldn't believe how scared he was. He'll never get out but would you like his autograph?"

Or just an attack of the tickles. Come up from behind and grab him, work fingers into the soft roll of the flesh popping up over his belt, a tummy filled with his mother's pasta. Put up with initial outrage until the kid decided to go with it and play. Tickle back until North allowed himself to be caught in a closet, on landings, up against the cellar door.

"What's it like?"

"What do you mean?"

"Being a masseuse."

"Oh, we don't call it that."

The men had returned to their chairs. Wynne's elbows were on the table and his head rested on the heels of his palms.

"That term is out of date. I'm a body therapist, I mean, I will be when I get my certificate. It's very rewarding, you know, to put people right. We learn to find tension spot and we put them right."

Wynne flashed a strange smile, composed of both smirk and contentment. "Well Pater," he said in a thick stagey voice, "what are you working on these days at the office? Still grabbing the small timers and missing crime in the suites? No executive privilege. Let's hear it."

"I'd love to tell you but you know there are confidentiality rules."

Wynne screwed up his face in rejection, but Sylvie saved North. She stuck her fist under his nose. "This is Silvie Capra for Channel Four here at the federal building where we are about to find out what's going on behind the scenes in the U.S. Attorney's office. Ok attorney North, give."

The easy give and take between Wynne and Sylvie both pained and sustained North. He had married two women without ever having held a conversation with himself or anyone else about his feelings. It was not that he didn't have affections; no one could call him cold. It was that he had never inquired what they were, much less their depth. It was as if someone had stuck a label on the relationship that announced "marriage means love," meaning he didn't have to travel beyond there. North could not believe two such savvy women had failed to tease this out, but he chased away the thought, thinking he was just dodging his own responsibility. While he was going to the South to express a way of being in the world that had seduced him, he was also a refugee, fleeing his failures with Susan and Diana, hoping distance would shred his memories.

This was North's moment. "The real news is I'm quitting. I meant to tell you earlier. I've decided to go to the South for a while. There's a need. Not sure when I'll be back. Come spring, Wynne, I'll expect you to mow the lawn. I've got to find a home for Graft. I doubt he can keep you company in a dorm."

"Going south?"

"Right away. Some details have to be worked out but I've given notice."

Wynne looked shocked. He looked down at his coffee cup. After a pause, he said, "Dad, you're doing good. I'm proud of you."

Autopsy

M cSorely learned more about what was going on when he met with Isadore Singer, the coroner. A strange duck.

McSorely'd checked Isadore out when he applied for the job. Dr. Izzy had gone to a good college near where he'd grown up in the Midwest and had graduated from Tulane Medical School in New Orleans with a decent record, specializing in pathology. He decided to stay in the South. Practiced in Baton Rouge for a while.

That was easy to document, but the whys were uncertain: the whys of him shortly leaving to work in another city in Louisiana and then for another job in Galveston, Texas, before he landed in Gulf City and as a pathologist at Davis Memorial. There was nothing in any police file about his background that suggested trouble: McSorely just assumed that he must have run into difficulties either because he might be a homosexual or because he was Jewish. Why the local medical establishment reputed to be so elitist and defensive of its historic privileges so readily approved a five foot two Jew who dressed poorly and who came without a wife was something of a mystery. He held a joint appointment—part time as the hospital pathologist, part time Gulf City medical examiner. The latter job had to mean there had been no resistance from the mayor, which also meant he was acceptable to the Posse.

As far as McSorely could tell, Dr. Izzy was not a social animal. At McSorely's wife's suggestion, even though she was still recovering from surgery, that a single man of the Hebrew extraction with two important jobs might be lonely, they had extended a dinner invitation, making sure he was told it would be a casual night. Without mentioning it to McSorely, his wife had also invited a widowed lady friend, but Singer found a lame excuse not to come. It's possible he was just the shy type.

Singer had long, bony hands that look powerful, the only part of his body that was impressive. He was not a man who bothered to shave every day. When as the chief of detectives, McSorely had business with the coroner, Singer greeted him warmly. He often told nonstop jokes that made McSorely laugh when he understood them. When he didn't, he'd bend down towards him, shading his face in a way that kept the pathologist from taking it in fully and McSorely tried to chuckle. "Ha, Ha," he might say in a stagey way more than once not to offend the man. "You are a card," he'd exclaim, just to keep things affable.

There was no denying the fact that like himself Singer was not Southern-born and for that reason alone McSorely guessed he tolerated, even liked, him. He was probably indulging in the fiction that their dual outlander status meant they were joined in knowing that the nonsense spewed by the local elite was, in fact, nonsense. Not that McSorely ever came out and actually said anything like that to him. That might have made it too real for comfort. And like a conspiracy. Police know the virtues of keeping one's mouth shut. But beyond this, McSorely only thought about such matters when an issue of consequence came up. He couldn't do his work otherwise.

Singer had taught McSorely indepth about autopsies, the kind of information a good chief in an area that has a remarkably high homicide rate should be well aware of. And he was grateful for McSorely's interest. The previous coroner, Doc Sargent, had vague contempt for anyone whose family couldn't trace its roots to before the War Between the States. He kept the police at arm's length until he reached his decision about the cause of death. And he did not take to a cop hovering near his makeshift morgue or at the funeral homes where the autopsies sometimes took place. Singer was different; he treated McSorely as a colleague in the world of forensic mysteries.

McSorely was no stranger to dead bodies, even misshapen, battered, twisted corpses that no one who didn't have to should ever view—but there was something different and disturbing in watching the coroner methodically slice down the front of the corpse like a butcher and remove the major organs, the brain and heart, and after sequestering tissue in plastic for later examination, replace them, close and suture the incision. All the while McSorely tried to ignore the foul smells that he knew would stay with him for the rest of the day. His wife was on the delicate side when it came to smells. She so detested the odor that she placed a large bar of strong laundry soap in the bathroom where he couldn't miss it.

The first time McSorely'd stood across a stone slab from Singer and watched him check the tissues, observe the arteries and look for signs of pathology—like tumors in the body of a young Black women who had her throat cut with what must have been something larger and a lot more-deadly than a kitchen knife—he thought of his own death. That night, he had an unsettling dream in which he was lying on the slab waiting for his own autopsy.

Of course, the procedure might be medically valuable, but not every death demanded one—the law's requirements depended on some suggestion of foul play or equally important suspicion or uncertainty—but McSorely knew it would be good for him to be present when Dr. Clem's took place, even as he silently noted that he was becoming squeamish. Not a good sign for the chief of detectives.

After McSorely briefed Singer on the known facts—the Browning Hi-Power 9mm caliber semiautomatic under her body, the dried blood, the crack in the window, the stone, and what looked to him like a bruise in the neck area—Singer finished the physical exam in a little less than an hour. His assistant brought McSorely coffee and him a Coke while he filled out paperwork that McSorely would pass on to Beau Cartwright, the District Attorney. Halfway through the forms, Singer was called away to take a phone call. When he came back to the small office next to the body room, McSorely noted that his manner was different. He still wrote with a pen but he pressed down hard on the paper as if he were wielding a hammer. He kept looking up as if he had something to say but then retreated to the forms. Finally, McSorely took the bait.

"So, Isadore, tell me." It hung in the air. McSorely could see he wasn't sure he should speak but then he just blurted it out.

"As you might have predicted, it was Ronson. He told me there was an explosion of gossip that had to be stopped before it impacted the wellbeing of the medical community and interfered with the hospital's application for federal money to fund the major expansion. Apparently, he'd learned things from two docs on the staff who had seen the body before it had been picked up from the funeral home. He'd talked by phone with your officer Pearson. It looked like an accident, he said, and you better get the word out without delay."

"Better ... or what?"

"Well, Ronson is a former flight surgeon, a military man history, I guess, and he certainly runs the hospital like a battalion commander. I have to make nice. I get this work because of him and I need it."

"You have some doubts?"

"A most complicated case. Clem was, of course, a provocative person. Everybody knows that. A woman in a man's world. Some people think she was involved with a civil rights lawyer named Chris North. Others were just scared of her. They suspected her racial views. It was thought by some, I understand, that she'd act on them—but that's not a matter of concern to me. I'm not a social analyst. I see a female in her forties, found dead on her front porch from what seems to be her own firearm. Your man found a cracked window and a rock nearby. It looks like she may have stumbled while investigating a burglary."

"And the bruise on her neck?"

"Have your people come up with any leads, suggestions of a burglary wave in the area?" McSorely knew instantly that Singer wasn't going to answer his question. "Any neighbors awakened?" he continued. "Did the stepfather hear anything? You know Mac, what her colleagues had against her most was not anything to do with race but her support for introduction of national standards coordination."

"What does that mean?"

"It's an evaluation program where our treatment records are compared with treatment records in other hospitals across the country. That's a challenge to the way things are done here; while it may be the future of medicine nationally, the docs here don't like it at all. The Davis staff does not trust what they'll hear from a bunch of Northern physicians who might have an axe to grind. They don't like Yankee interference. It's feared this sort of thing may lead to socialized medicine."

"Ok, ok, I understand, let's keep politics out of this. If you come up with anything that might change what happens down the road, let me know. But more important is what the physical evidence shows."

Singer nodded. He looked down at the forms in front of him and rubbed his eyes with a thumb and forefinger. "Of course, Mac, of course. Give my regards to your wife. I haven't yet decided. I'll let you know."

"Of course, meaning what?"

"Meaning I may want to see if the City will pay for an outside consultant."

"Ah, a buffer."

"If you want to call it that. It's a long shot. Bunch of cheapskates in this town when it comes hiring external experts. As I said, there is fear they'll be subject to prejudice because they are from the South."

Two days later, Singer's assistant delivered the report to McSorely as chief of detectives. The finding was "Death by accident." There was no call for an outside consultant. He was not surprised. But here was a white woman. A woman with an incontrovertible reputation for unsettling the City fathers. A lady doctor. Something was out of place. Death threats maybe. Car tires punctured. Feces sent through the mail. He'd even seen offal smeared on doors and a noose sent to a white lawyer who represented a Black man charged with raping a white woman. But no, he just didn't think the Sheets would do this. At least not on their own. But then who? Because to someone who could never shake being a Jersey guy, he thought calling the death an accident was pure bullshit.

But McSorely put his doubts aside. Finding out more wouldn't come from the order in which events happened. He could ask questions but in this mosaic the pattern would be a broken one. The colors random. Lines crossed. There'd be no straight answers. It didn't matter. Things being the way they were, he wasn't going to ask. No one to wiretap. No prints. If he found out, it would have to come to him. A visit from the great God informer. Maybe tomorrow. Certainly not today. He told himself *stay tuned, stay tuned Mac.*

North to South

North tried to sign on at first with one of the lawyer groups that were flooding the Deep South that summer to support civil rights workers, but his first attempt was a failure. He first reached a secretary. Expecting immediate deference, he made it clear he was calling from the U.S. Attorney's office. He was transferred to a familiar voice, a guy on leave from a white-shoe Boston firm who was coordinating volunteers as a pro bono project.

The lawyer turned out to have defended a corporate client North had prosecuted a few years earlier on a charge of bribing a foreign government official to get preferential treatment for a contract to build a dam on some Asian river. Once he realized who it was on the phone, the lawyer wanted to rehash the plea deal he hadn't liked. North just listened to his grievance, let him mouth off and finally couldn't take it anymore. He told the lawyer—whose name and face but not his voice he had forgotten—to take a long walk on a short pier, and hung up.

Pretty stupid on my account, he told himself. *If I want to change I better start being different.* Later, when he knew more about himself he thought, *well, I was in my self-righteous saving-the-Negro*

24

period; I must have believed in my sainthood. How could anyone not just welcome and cherish my sacrifice, put everything else aside and worship the purity of my white soul? North had been secretly reading self-help books, and meditating in his office for short periods when he was sure no one would notice. He blamed being a prosecutor for the disarray of his feelings. He rarely lost a case, but, paradoxically, winning led him to question a life spent putting people in prison, not all of them by any means public enemy number one, two or three. Doubts could not be discussed with his colleagues. He'd tried once to broach the subject with a veteran prosecutor who had taught him much about plea bargaining when he joined the office, but it was obvious after a few stumbling sentences that he wasn't being heard, so he beat a hasty retreat. As his sense of dislocation deepened, North decided there was more to it than typical lawyer burnout. He tried to meditate but couldn't let the world around him go away. He took a power yoga class but his body, coming off too many years sitting at a desk, refused to bend. Nevertheless, after disregarding the instructor's insistence that Downward Facing Dog would lead to spiritual peace, he decided that only an act of will would get him straightened out. North understood that his commitment to going south was as much for him as his clients to be.

Frustrated after this disconnect, he called his college roommate, Sal Ferretti, for advice. Sal had moved from practicing internal medicine at Johns Hopkins to a big administrative job in the government that North thought had something to do with the way the health care system dealt with poor people as well as race issues in hospitals. Maybe he would have a lead. Dr. Sal was quick to tell him that taking care of the medically indigent was only a small part of what he did—*pretty closed mouthed*, North thought, *the way he said it*—but after hearing North tell him he wanted to make a big change in his life, Ferretti grew less reticent, became more the easygoing comrade of too many college binge-drinking escapades. Ferretti confided that while not much was happening right then, there was a big lawsuit and a civil rights law that might change things.

They talked about other stuff for a while—North's women problems, why he felt he could no longer be a prosecutor; Sal's wife and his kids. He told North his children were thriving. He was happy his son Tony seemed to have escaped the Vietnam War draft but he was afraid Serena was having trouble adapting to what was going on in the world. Maybe it was early menopause. Then abruptly he changed the subject back to North's reason for calling. He wondered whether Tony could help. The boy had taken a leave from Columbia with a group of fellow students to help start a kind of underground newspaper in Gulf City, Alabama, that was supposed to cover civil rights movement stories that the established press wouldn't touch. Even if the big papers ran a piece, the students feared it might be shallow, avoiding what was really going on. Gulf City had avoided the fullscale demonstrations and violence of Montgomery and Birmingham but little more had happened than token moves toward integration. Tony told him the public schools were still segregated; few skilled jobs had been offered to African Americans. Instead of "segregation forever" talk from officials and tear gas from the police, Gulf City business leaders were adept at cooling things down with mostly symbolic changes.

Tony's group had persuaded one of their dads, a Wall Street trader, to set them up. That was how North eventually found himself at an empty desk in a mothballed old factory building near the docks that the students had rented with contributions from the investor and a grant to put out the paper from a small Westchester County family foundation.

Ferretti's son, North thought, was mature for his age. A kick ass kid, sprouting long sideburns and a bushy mustache, dressed in the type of cool blue overalls favored by French workers that had been picked up by civil rights activists. Walking around Gulf City, he had the look of a foreign invader. He didn't seem to notice the hostile glances from people passing him on the streets. Tony was quick to exploit his father's former roommate's desire to get involved and floated a plan right away.

Tony supposed folks who needed legal help would be drawn to the paper to tell their stories; by being near the reporters, North could start getting known by offering free legal advice. Even though he would be practicing law without an Alabama license, he probably could get away with it until he had to go to court. By then, Tony thought, he might be able to get help by partnering with local Black lawyers. It turned out pretty much as Tony had imagined because within a few months North had a local reputation as a go to guy who also charged little or nothing, which in turn brought him to the attention of the most prominent African American lawyer in the City.

Orzell Williams had, of course, an Alabama law license, but not a lot of the federal court experience. Orzell was an education for North, as well as entry into the local activist community; in turn, North was a source for the federal court way of doing things for the Alabamian. Williams, as everybody who is familiar with civil rights history knows, died years later when his car jumped a guardrail and ended up in a creek on the less populated east side of the bay that defined the shape of the City. Some thought that what the police called a tragic accident had been engineered by the Klan. The findings of an FBI report on the crash requested by the NAACP were inconclusive. If there was a culprit, the government had failed to find him. But Orzell was very much alive when they first met. The key for North was that from the start they could say anything to each other.

In the weeks following Orzell's death, North found himself holding conversations with him in his head. He had an almost physical sense that part of him had been amputated by his death. There was plenty of reason to hold onto suspicions about the way Orzell died. But North had never been completely persuaded by the Klan story. While it was certainly possible—his wife, Marcella, had said her husband had more death threats than paper clips in his top desk drawer—and it was well known that shots had been fired into their house several times. Once, a bomb had destroyed the sleeping porch. Still North's hunch was that the culprit was more likely too much moonshine or maybe even Cutty Sark, Orzell's favorite Scotch.

But they would have years together as partners, for which North, who put down roots in Gulf City, was grateful. When they met, Orzell was one of the few attorneys who would take civil rights cases anywhere near the City; if you drew a broad circle around the area where he had an office it could be labeled O.W. territory. Aside from Movement cases, he'd been the lawyer of choice in countless broken marriages, custody battles, drug prosecutions, sexual assaults, rape and murder charges. In his office, he'd witnessed the stories of families coming apart, police beating his neighbors, white farmers cheating their tenants, lots of raging Black men, all manner of drunks and hatred. Even by what he regarded as his own community, he'd been threatened, told he was an Uncle Tom by some young activists and a communist by others as well as a destroyer of Black teacher jobs by seeking integration of the schools. In unguarded moments, he'd tell North that what bothered him most was not the criticism but the personal tragedies he had witnessed. The men and women who had been unable to accept who they were; who deep down saw themselves as they were viewed by the bigots, a step that all too often led to depression or even craziness.

"That was the worst," he declaimed after one of his many lectures to North on "How race has fucked us up."

If you filed as many lawsuits as Orzell, you'd make some friends but even more enemies; and even more likely than enemies, your daily constant would be stress. Too often, there was nothing Orzell could do but listen and sympathize. That's hard on a lawyer, North knew. It takes a toll. "We're trained to *do*," O.W. would say, not just talk. He complained he had too good a memory. Why couldn't he forget more? North thought his brain must have been filled with a record of human misery his new partner couldn't abide but also couldn't let slip away. Orzell lacked a talent for selective amnesia.

It was in Orzell's downtown office, a shabby second floor space above a Krispy Kreme bakeshop, where North first saw her. Where life took him over with a mind of its own. In North's windowless, closet-sized workspace, the walls covered with smashed carcasses of dead insects, he was writing part of a brief for Orzell in a case challenging the City's closing of voter registration offices in Negro areas. Marcella, who sometimes served as Orzell's secretary, put her head in the room to say he wanted North to come to his office right away —another small room facing a rubble-filled backyard always inundated with a sweet smell from the pastry ovens below.

In the office, there was no room for another place to sit, so North stood to the side of O.W.'s chair and felt his lungs drain of air. Did he know her or was it just a resemblance? Seated next to a haggard-looking Black woman who turned out to be her housekeeper, she gave no sign of recognition. For some reason he could not trace, North immediately concluded that the housekeeper had brought her up. They were there because the Black woman's grandson had been busted on drug-selling charges—it was heroin—by the feds. Orzell wanted North to explain to them why the kid, he was just nineteen, had to plead guilty. But before North could say anything, she talked about the injustice of the sentence the boy had been offered. The grandmother interjected that he was just holding a package for a friend but mostly it was the white woman who did the talking.

Her voice was a familiar but North couldn't be sure. She wore what he realized was a white lab coat over the kind of patterned shirtwaist dress white Southern women seemed to favor. Later, of course, he learned her whole story, but then he pushed away the thought that they were in college together.

North took refuge from his confusion by delivering a standard lecture about the necessities of plea bargaining, almost as if he were talking to a tape recorder. When he paused, she jumped in to say how stupid it was to send the young man away for five years where he would spend his time warehoused with hardened criminals when even if he wasn't innocent she could get him a job as an apprentice at her hospital. She would train him to do work attending to some of her aged patients.

North barely heard her argument. But he kept his eyes on hers and nodded as if he was listening carefully. He was elsewhere. Not only was she beautiful, she was a filled-out grown woman like Susan, who talked with the sort of command that reminded him of Diana. *This woman knows herself* was the thought that came to him. She was composed in a way that suggested she was grounded in her own security. But he realized he had better be careful, that he was a bigtime loser when it came to first-sight female impressions. It also came to him more powerfully that he must have seen a much younger version.

After she finished what he heard as a mini-sermon, North tried again to explain the logic of what they faced with a federal drug charge: "We can try to get a better deal but he has to plead. There is no way he was going to beat the charge, not in this city or probably not anywhere in the U.S.A., and after a loss at trial—when not if—the court will more or less double the sentence."

Her eyes met North's for the first time but he thought that was because she didn't like what she heard. He was certain she wouldn't like any messenger who delivered this message. He was glad Orzell hadn't mentioned what work he used to do. Plainly, he'd been brought into the room to take her heat; through the whole thing Orzell hadn't said a word. He mostly studied his tie like it was a passage from the Bible. North figured he'd never see her again. Probably a good thing, he was sure, given his track record. But what then about the scent of familiarity? And why had he never asked her name?

Had they been to college together, even in a class or two? He'd have to ask Ferretti; maybe he'd remember her. North had had a scholarship deal that allowed him meals for no cost if he washed dishes four days and two nights a week. Women lived at the Roman Hall Co-op, a rambling Victorian pile surrounded by stately trees that were dying from Dutch Elm Disease, but men could sign up to eat there. Kitchen jobs were parceled out by a senior named Newhouse. Nobody ever called him by a first name if they even knew it. Newhouse had a title, "Head Coordinator." He drove a battered white van that he used to scour the farms in the rural area that surrounded the college town for bargains. He was wiry but muscular. Looked as if he worked out with weights. He filled out the tight blue chambray work shirt he wore every day under floppy overalls. As North watched him on Fall days unloading bags of sweet corn at the back of the kitchen, he wondered if Newhouse owned a dozen versions of this uniform or simply wore the same shirt and overall combination again and again.

She waitressed, if it was her, and he saw her and she him when she dumped garbage in the cans next to the big porcelain sink at which he handwashed dishes, scrubbed grease and food scraps from pots and pans. She would stack the dirty plates where he could get them and turn away without a word.

He had taken her measure too often for comfort. She was solid, he thought, like a tree that moved; dressed in a way to suggest she wanted to hide the size of her breasts. She wore large framed tortoiseshell glasses that made it hard to see her eyes. Thinking of acid comments his mother often made about some of her friends, he wondered if a woman like her would turn to fat or flab when she got older. But the decisive way she moved, the way she handled the heavy trays, made him think she'd never succumb to any purely physical weakness. He pondered whether he had the courage to ask her out but then one day he saw her riding across the campus with Newhouse, his van filled for the Co-op with crates of fresh fruits and vegetables, industrial size cans of tomatoes, one or two of lard. She seemed to be smiling. Happy. That was it. He'd just have to forget her.

Doctor Clem

Like a mind-sticker song, North's thoughts turned to her those few hours when he wasn't doing law. Once North was sure he saw Clem at a barbeque place near Jackson, Mississippi, where he'd gone to meet with a newly minted lawyer, the first Black to graduate from a Southern State law school, but when the woman turned in his direction, she was so clearly someone else that he was embarrassed.

He had to see her; to find out if she was who he thought she was, but for weeks his trials and travel made it impossible. And he realized he still didn't even know her name.

It happened weeks later in the emergency room at a shabby medical clinic near the Alabama Georgia border. The rights group in a nearby town had gone through the proper motions, applying for a permit for a street march to demonstrate against the Jim Crow segregation enforced by almost every business on Main Street. Of course, it was denied. Usually towns gave phony but superficially plausible reasons for saying no to permission to march—too much traffic, too much noise, or they would announce how they were strongly against litter dirtying the streets and so forth—but this time the mayor and town council didn't even bother. They just said *no way*. North had gone to federal court with a claimed denial of free speech and assembly rights and came out with a standard court order allowing peaceful picketing and marching if the traffic wasn't impeded.

A local group called the Negro Civic League had sought the permit and its leadership was unsurprised at the rejection. The members were middle-aged: a few teachers in the still-segregated public schools, a woman who nursed the elderly, a Methodist pastor, and two federal employees from the post office. A former coal miner named Willis Hampton was local leader of the group and, at first, he counseled his forty or so members that they had to talk through the issues; then they would seek a meeting with the mayor.

When the mayor refused the meeting, Hampton sought the help of SNCC, the Student Nonviolent Coordinating Committee, in Atlanta. They sent one of their field secretaries, a college-age Kentuckian named Rashad Forbush, to advise the League. Meanwhile the Methodist pastor welcomed a white Unitarian minister from Rhode Island as a visiting preacher. At a community meeting, Forbush vehemently urged the League to march anyway; the pastor and the Northern minister thought it would be better to go back to the mayor first. Forbush viciously attacked them as cowards afraid to challenge the racist establishment. Hampton tried to mediate but the meeting ended without a resolution. He contacted Orzell Williams for advice and Orzell sent North to consult with the group. North agreed to stop off at the town on his way to a court date in Albany, Georgia. But before he could arrive, Forbush persuaded the group to march. He told the members that lawyers were of no use once direct action is called for. Hampton had left school to go to work when he was twelve but he was a real spellbinder when he had something to say. Bowing to pressure from Forbush, he used the court decision as a way to push his followers into action: "The judge has told us citizens we can exercise our rights to march and so we have to follow his lead. And we are tired of waiting."

The following day, Hampton and Forbush led about two-dozen demonstrators on the banned march down the town's Main Street. They sang freedom songs and held anti-segregation signs. Black kids on bikes rode past retail stores and lobbed leaflets at the front doors. White passersby mostly scattered but a few picked up the leaflets and tossed them away. The mayor had called in the state police but they stayed on the edge of town, at a distance from the demonstrators. The troopers displayed riot gear in a way that suggested they might step in at any time.

Hampton finally stopped the group at Courthouse Square, directly in front of the granite facade of the National Bank. Standing on a packing box before the marchers, he reached down to put his arm around Forbush, then introduced him as a freedom fighter from Atlanta. The marchers crowded closer to the bank entrance so they could hear as the SNCC worker began to speak. Hampton stood slightly behind him to the left. His body suddenly twisted toward the ground like corkscrew, his head swung to the side, has eyes buggy. He had no idea what had hit him but North knew immediately Hampton had been shot. North had ridden with enough cops on night patrols when he was a student in a criminal law training program and also on a year as a prosecutor in Brooklyn. He was standing next to his car watching the march and he immediately stepped back behind the wheel and drove the car toward Hampton as fast as he could, parting the bodies in front of him and then pulling the man in the backseat, his face still contorted, blood creeping along the side of his jeans.

There she was standing at the door of a makeshift treatment room at a clinic a mile out of town. She paid North no mind, as if she had never seen him before. He was directed to a tiny waiting room while two Black women lifted Hampton on a gurney taking him out of sight. North found a phone. After he tried unsuccessfully to reach an FBI agent in Atlanta to get the Bureau to intervene, he found a chair in the waiting room. A half hour later, one of the women shook a dozing North on the shoulder to tell him that Doctor Clem wanted him to know that the patient was out of danger.

Later, in her motel room, Clem is talking to the man she will come to love. North has been told not to interrupt. He does his best.

Clem says, "You want to know my story; say about who influenced me. I could point to a couple of teachers, especially an art instructor in high school. He taught at our very exclusive, we were always told, private school only three years but I had him for two courses, art history and a studio course in drawing. He saw something in me that I didn't see in myself. I was totally confused, and didn't get it, even thought he had an ulterior motive—though he never got physically close. He wasn't that sort of man. He might have even been a homosexual but at the time, like most people, I was clueless about that."

"Don't you think," North asked, "the way this works is if somebody you respect thinks you are valuable you end up believing it?"

"Oh, I agree. He talked a lot about, well, just history, and I lapped it up. American history that isn't in the textbooks, not only about art though he used the story behind paintings to get there, like what he said about George Washington having his inserted false teeth pulled from the mouths of his slaves. Can you believe that? But let me go on.

"I began to feel there was a reason—though I couldn't tell you then or maybe even now what it was—that I was not anything like the girls I grew up with. No Southern Belle, white gloved, sugar and spice for me. I don't think I ever wore a taffeta dress."

"Were you rebellious?"

"Not at all. Just thought I was a bit of a tomboy; I liked sports. I liked science. I had friends and took my schooling seriously. But my kin went all the way back, and while my mom never talked much about it, there were slave owners and a cotton warehouse owner in her ancestry. My father was a lawyer and the son of a lawyer and he inherited a practice representing shipping companies in Gulf City, New Orleans, and Mobile. I don't remember him well because he died young of a mysterious illness. But my mother, when she drank more sherry than she could handle, would reminisce, always beginning with how handsome he was, how hard he worked, and if she really was into it running on about his favorite Italian suits and ties.

"While I certainly didn't think of it at the time, it's possible I became a doctor because on some crazy level I wanted to save people from my father's fate but, of course, that's the kind of murky thinking that might be true but also is totally unverifiable and my adult life has been all about verification. Though I have to admit there's a lot we don't know, a lot we have to guess. You know, like it or not, when you are guessing over people's lives or fooling with their bodies you don't feel much like a noble scientist."

"I feel like I'm interviewing you," North interjected, "but I'd like to know what the war was like for you."

"I guess I have to go into that. Some of what happened in the war I shouldn't be telling you or anyone for that matter. I never have before. But in a certain sense that might shock you—don't push me on this just listen—it all has to come out. Given what we do we have so little time for each other. By the way, I need the same openness from you.

"Anyway, coming out of our college, I went to a nursing school in Boston but after the introductory courses I was solicited to join the U.S. Army. A recruiter came through and offered a small bonus. The backstory was that the country was running out of men for all sorts of wartime military support roles. They'd created a Women's Auxiliary Corps and were in the process of converting it to put women in real army positions. But all hell broke loose when it was announced with conservatives giving out, believe it or not, that females had to stay on the homefront. The Auxiliary Corps members were of loose morals, they got pregnant or gave the troops what today we call STDs; and a regular army Women's Corp would undermine the soldiers—you know they wouldn't be focused on killing or something like that. So, anyway, while General George Marshall, who was the military boss, got what he wanted in setting up the Woman's Army Corps, the members of the Auxiliary voted with their feet not to transfer to it. They didn't want to be slandered as whorish or whatever names were being called.

"That's why I was recruited. I could have stayed in nursing school and then served because it was the one job that women could hold that escaped all the debate. I guess it was ok to let females empty bedpans or minister to the dying, but I accepted the new assignment.

"I'll try to keep the rest of the story shorter though it is where the change in me took place, both as a physical person and a doctor person. Are you bored?"

"Go on please. Given our work lives, this is a rare opportunity."

"Well you seem to be listening and you aren't interrupting—well not too much. I have to admit I like that, though this could become a monologue. I haven't told the whole story to anyone else. I'm still wondering why you. Maybe it's that you are not from here, you're sort of out of network, and that's a comfort. Maybe it's that I had a crush on you at school. Of course, you wouldn't have any idea of that because it embarrassed me as it was based on fantasy. I did nothing about it then and I don't know what will happen to us now. For all I know we may never get together. I'm certainly not saying I want that but if it happens you'll have carried the story far away, which is good; I'll have gotten it out of my system, which is also good. Maybe I'm telling you just because we knew each other in college. At least, by a lot of looks. I'm not sure you are aware of what your looks conveyed. Or maybe I'm telling because deep down, in a place I won't admit is there, I still have hopes for a normal life.

"From that look on your face I can tell you weren't sure I remembered. Of course, I knew right away that day you came into lawyer Williams's office. I don't share much in the way of personal information around here and around here is where I live and work and will stay. I don't do a lot of trusting, except in the evidence I use when I'm diagnosing. You see I'm out of phase. Not of this place because I feel *dis*placed when I'm not here but of its view of the world. What I remember most is that when we both worked in the dining hall kitchen, I dumped the dishes next to you. When you glanced in my direction, I saw you had lovely blue eyes."

"I wanted to get to know you," North interjected, "but in those days I wasn't sure how to do it. Then there was Newhouse. You seemed to be spoken for."

"Let's leave all that behind; it's not important anymore and I want to get back to the story. The reason I'm telling you all this I suppose is it explains why I'm a doctor; maybe why I do what I do, which is still another story. Anyway, I was inducted and quickly sent to Fort Monmouth in Jersey; told I was a clerk-typist and assigned to the staff of a colonel in the Signal Corps. Let's just call him Richard. He was about twenty years older than I was but actually just in his forties. Very distinguished looking. Married with a couple of young children. I never met his family. He rarely mentioned them but there was a photograph on his desk of them all sitting at a picnic table. The kids, a boy and a girl, were looking straight into the camera but his wife had her face to the side as if she didn't really want to have her picture taken. It was not the face of a happy person. He had an engineering background and was all work; for a career soldier amazingly open, even sweet, not one of the by-the-book rigid types you usually think of in his job, which was to over-see aspects of telephonic communications in the upcoming invasion of the Italian mainland.

"I fell totally in love with him. I'd never met a man who was or at least seemed so secure. Never put anyone down. He treated me as a regular person not some gal who had landed from another planet in his war. He was a just-get-the-job-done kind of guy. When a member of his staff screwed up or there were delays in getting equipment we needed into the pipeline, he tried to solve the problem. Never blamed. I can't say at that time he knew how much I was mooning over him, but when our group was ordered to Tunisia to set up a Corps Headquarters for the Salerno invasion, what was called Operation Avalanche in Army code gobbledygook, he took me with him.

"And that's when it got complicated. The work was extraordinarily demanding as you can imagine. Communications for the troops after they reached the beach was mostly by wire-supported field telephones. Radio wasn't much trusted because the Germans figured out your position when you used it. The phones in question had been around for a while; back then they were even carried by soldiers in a leather or canvas bag which was supposed to help keep the D-cell batteries dry. The equipment was essential for communication among the upfront units and, of course, for reports back to command posts. They depended, believe it or not, on wire that Signal Corps G.I.s had to lay by hand between platoons moving up to front lines and back to a command post. From there the wires had to reach even back to Regimental HQs where there were often switchboards, a whole other can of worms. Laying the wires was dangerous, out in the open, work; there was digging, in places, and covering gullies with earth. There was lethal strafing from German planes. Often our own armor or jeeps would run over and cut a newly placed wire and the Signal Corps guys would have to go back and repair the line. Many of them died doing the kind of work we see every day here from Southern Bell repairmen. These guys were courageous but they were also sitting ducks."

"I never realized that women were involved doing the work you're describing. Were you alone?"

"As reports of what was happening to our guys came in, I had to keep from crying. It was hard enough being a woman in our section without me going soft in front of men who wouldn't let their emotions show. There were no other females on the operational side in Richard's section."

"Did you feel isolated?"

"I had a few incidents that I could call harassment—one from the major who was Richard's second in command—but I was protected by male privilege. Most of the guys who might have come after me assumed I was Richard's mistress, his property not theirs, or else why was I there? Actually, there was little time for such games in the Summer and Fall of 1943. Salerno was ultimately a successful landing but the Germans had almost overrun the beaches by splitting U.S. troops from the British invasion force. I don't know what saved Avalanche from disaster but I know that once the beaches were secure our work became more important. My role was to get the field wire not only ordered but actually delivered to where it was supposed to go and also to make sure there were ways to explain the equipment to enlisted men pressed into service who had no experience with telephone work. Here I was sitting in Tunis, and later Algiers, with equipment manuals, talking to men on the mainland of Italy about connectors and switchboards. God knows what else, as if I was Alexander Graham Bell. I read the manuals at night and repeated what they said the next day trying to sound like an expert. When I told Richard that I felt like a fraud, he put his hand on my shoulder, touching me for the first time. He just said, 'It's the war. It's the way we all feel if we're honest about it.'

"After the army finally took Naples, I was sent to the mainland. We supported the soldiers as they moved north toward Rome through well-defended valleys and mountains. It was a brutal campaign. Deadly battles like Monte Cassino and San Pietro are well-known but they were just two among dozens. San P. is interesting because it became a movie, a documentary full of death and emotion that was later called a fake because the famous director used too much footage that came from other battles. But forgive me, I digress. I'm back in my head."

"Are you going to tell me what happened with you and Richard?"

"Christopher, I think I'll understand the question as a tiny expression of jealousy. That pleases me."

"Putting it that way is a turn on. It's almost like foreplay."

"You've been patient, so I will give you an answer, but I also want to close this out. The Army had more trouble with communications as it approached Rome. Richard was deployed near the front lines. We had become close in the months we were stuck in North Africa but we never had a physical relationship. To be honest, I think we were on the verge when he left. He was the very opposite of a man who comes on to you; in fact, he let his feelings be known by exposing his sadness. There was something in his marriage that I think was poisonous, but he was too loyal to his wife or maybe self-protective to be specific about that. I wasn't totally inexperienced but I was young and this downside of him, one he showed me but no one else, made me want to be even closer to him.

"But then he was gone. One day the Army ordered him to England, for what must have been pre-D-Day work. I never saw him again. We exchanged a few letters and I learned after the war that he had moved to the desert near Tucson. When he left, I was suddenly exposed in a terrible way. The skirt whose guy has left her is open season. The major and then a few others in different ways, some approaching violence and other just verbally strident, tried to bed me. I had to be careful and savvy to keep safe but when it seemed impossible just to do my job I wangled a transfer to the nursing corps, and eventually was assigned to a hospital in Maryland. I was there a while, that led to a med school and the rest as they say, don't they, is history."

"Can I ask another question?"

"Go ahead."

"Why did you come back to Gulf City? You'd lived in a different way; seen all kinds of people. You came back to a place that was probably backward by the standards of where you'd been and what you as a woman had done."

"It's the right question. But during the War, Gulf City was transformed. People flooded in for the shipbuilding jobs. They built a huge airbase out of town. Even though there were riots, I'd heard African Americans were for the first time being offered skilled jobs. A few women were even hired as welders on the condition they find a way to get trained. I didn't think hard about it. Should have. Just expected we'd join the rest of the country but I was wrong.

"The truth is that why I came back after medical school and residency in Boston is a question I try to avoid. I always put it on my mother needing me. She has blood issues and they need to be watched. It could be the kind of leukemia that doesn't kill you—at least right away–but has to be treated. I've told this story so often I almost believe it but in fact mother's condition would wax or wane regardless of where I practiced medicine.

"A more tangled truth worried me; that I'd come home because the competition would be easier. I would stand out in the South but in Boston or Philadelphia be just one of a crowd of agonizingly and carefully trained doctors of medicine, a cohort that had been told it was going to change the face of treatment across the board in the years to come. It would be hard for a woman anywhere but I decided maybe the toughness of my wartime experience would get me through more easily where I'd grown up, a place where I knew instinctively how you got to be one of the players. And as a woman I'd be unusual; I'd stand out! There was the matter of charm, of deportment. It worked in the South if you know how to use it; in Boston somehow that sort of stuff gets lost. In Gulf City, people smile at you and say good morning if they pass you on the street. Boston is a place where people physically fight over parking places.

"It took a year for me to admit the real reason for returning was Richard, my wartime boss. I wanted to see him again and while he was in Arizona, not Gulf City, I thought it more likely we would meet if I moved home. A fantasy, yes; for a time, I felt desperate. But the need for him faded when I confronted the reality of practicing medicine. I like to think I became a grownup those first few months. Still, nothing worked out the way I expected."

"Something radicalized you."

"But, at first, I thought I could get along with the old boy network that controlled all but the woeful municipal clinic that treated

African Americans and others not deemed worthy or wealthy enough to be admitted to Davis Memorial. Given where I'd been and what I knew I just couldn't contain myself at medical society and hospital staff meetings. Even though I'd been welcomed, I felt it was a superficial niceness. The medical community had its way of doing things: I should be grateful that I was now a member of the anointed few. That gratitude involved not questioning the traditional arrangements—shelving concerns about the health of the community as a whole. Or pointing out the changes happening nationally in treatment and public health best practices was too often scorned, if even attended to, by my colleagues. What bothered me most was the way the powers that be viewed the poor, white or Black, but especially the health needs of minorities. I started out thinking that by coming home to the segregated South, I had to accept the terms and conditions of its way of life. But too much had happened to me in Italy, in northern ERs, in surgery rotations as an intern watching bodies come in with gunshots, from terminal cancer patients and the drip, drip, drip of patients' end of life sagas, to pretend I could live in a bubble of country club medicine.

"Two incidents—one predictable, the other tragic—drove me into the arms of personal opposition.

"Doctor Manny Dupre is an African American pediatrician, the only one in Gulf City. Much in demand in his community, certified in his specialty by the appropriate national board, he's a totally non-political animal. His sister, Marcella, is the wife of your law partner. Orzell Williams is a controversial figure in Gulf City, hated and loved. Manny is different; a laidback, serious scientist. He applied to the Gulf City chapter of the state medical society to be able to attend the society-sponsored monthly lecture series that brings in speakers to talk about new developments in medicine. He had no interest in socializing with its all-white membership and less in futilely applying for staff membership at Davis Memorial—even when a child in his care required admission to the hospital for specialized treatment and he had to turn his patient over to a white doctor with staff admitting privileges. If the right treatment was available, he could use a small hospital in the suburbs built and staffed by a religious order of the Catholic Church. At least then he could stay connected to his patient. Another option was a modern facility in Tuskegee funded by the federal government that was only supposed to serve veterans but occasionally it made exceptions. But he rarely used Tuskegee. Even if the hospital would take the child, its location was really too far away for family members to visit."

"I can see what's coming."

"Not only was his application to attend the Society lectures series denied, it was not really discussed. What I heard from colleagues was a few brief doublespeak comments. But one from the white pediatrician who regularly took over patients from Dr. Dupre so they could be admitted to Davis was remarkably frank: he said that if the colored doctor moved up in the pecking order and ultimately used Society membership as a foothold to gain admitting privileges at Davis, his own income would be seriously impacted. The only other comment I remember was from the Society president, the reigning chief at Davis, Hedley Ronson, who said no formal vote on the application was necessary as it was obvious it would be unanimously rejected. Ronson told us that big changes 'along these lines' were being hatched in Washington and the Society, as the voice of medical quality in Gulf City and surrounding areas, needed toughness to protect its prerogatives as keepers of the Hippocratic Oath.

"I was about to speak before Ronson abruptly moved down the agenda, but the words wouldn't come. They tumbled from my mind to my throat but lay there weighed down by anger and, I have to admit, fear. When I brought the news to Manny, expecting fury and bitterness, he thanked me for my support, betrayed no emotion and only said, 'What did you expect?'

"The second incident took place months later, when I felt more settled in my choice to return to Gulf City. I not only took a position but provoked as much by the way I did it as that I did it. An African American teenager had shoplifted two bags of potato chips from an Eastside mini-market. The employee at the checkout, also African American, had confronted him. The boy brandished a knife. The employee pulled a gun from behind the counter and shot the boy twice, then calmly called the police and told them to order an ambulance. The boy was taken to Davis Memorial but the Emergency Room refused to treat him, directing the driver, who was new, in strong language to the municipal clinic. When they got there, the boy was DOA.

"I came to the Society meeting the next week with a written resolution directed to all Gulf City medical facilities urging that emergency cases should be admitted immediately on the basis of patient condition regardless of 'social' and other factors. I came to the meeting room early, laid copies of the resolution on the chairs and the desk from which Ronson would chair the meeting. After the usual anteroom chatter over white wine and canapes that proceeded the formal gathering, the members entered the meeting room glanced at the paper and turned silent. When Ronson spoke, he thanked me by name—'our newly arrived colleague straight from Boston'—for my 'humanitarian' efforts and then said 'But, of course, we don't deal with political matters.' He crumpled the paper and put it aside.

"Scared as I was, I took a deep breath, stood and looking straight at him said, 'Dr. Ronson, I would like the sense of the meeting on this.' Ronson again offered thanks for my concern but he ignored my request. He moved to the first item on the agenda which had to do with raising dues for the next fiscal year. I looked around at my colleagues hoping for support but no one looked back.

"It was only then that I fully understood what it was like to be alone. I had to choose to stay or go and if I stayed I'd have to do something. Whatever 'something' meant at the time I had no idea but soon I took a small step—seems so piddling but it shocked many—I let white and Black patients sit together in my private office waiting room. My receptionist quit. I lost a few patients, but at least I'd broken out of the vacuum."

Mister Why Are You Here?

When North set up shop with Orzell Williams, he suddenly became known in Gulf City and its surrounds. He also was available to a network of local and regional civil rights groups that were largely invisible to the mainstream media, even to national organizations like the NAACP Legal Defense Fund and the Congress of Racial Equality. He bought a used Chevrolet because it had noticeable dents and carried Alabama plates. At Orzell's suggestion, North stuck a "Go Tide" football support sticker on the back bumper to advertise local ties. He put over 3,000 miles on the car in the first two months, travelling a route from Gulf City to Mississippi Delta towns like Greenville to conservative cities well to the east like Macon, Georgia.

He had a rented room in Gulf City, but was rarely there. When northern-based legal groups asked him to take on the cases of demonstrators arrested in towns far from Orzell's office, he would end up sleeping in extra rooms at the houses of his clients' families. The neighbors would look at him strangely at first, then after inquiring about who he was of his hostess—usually a church affiliated Black woman, who often displayed grandmotherly attentions like introducing him to a breakfast of proper grits—they would treat him with an elaborate courtesy. There were others, usually young Black civil rights workers, who didn't mind when he went to court for them but weren't sure of his attachment.

North was pleased with his legal work but he had no illusions about what he accomplished. Trying cases before local judges was usually arguing to a brick wall, but at least he made a record that might support a successful appeal. There were, however, times where his persistence paid off. He would assert a series of procedural errors or slip in any delaying tactics he could come up with to create such annoyance in the local law enforcers that often the prosecution got set aside or even dismissed.

"As a lawyer," North said to his partner, "I've been protected so far from the harassment and intimidation I expected."

"I'll forgive you," Orzell responded, "because it is not because you are a lawyer but 'cause you are a *white* lawyer you haven't encountered the stuff I have to deal with all the time. You have just a month on the hustings in some small, backward towns. A lot of churchy ladies making you soul food. Listen, you're doing good work. It is most valuable. But just you wait. The kids will test you. The supremacists will be nothing compared to the kids from my side of the street. Just you wait till the SNCC workers go after you. You are still whitey. They wouldn't be saying white North *bad*; it's more complicated. They will treat you like you are a doting mom who is starting to micromanage their life—'Why don't you do this, not that?' And so forth.

"'Mister,' they'll say, or maybe just think, 'Why are you here and for how long?'"

North was brought up short. Understanding for the first time that while the racists were a constant, more important at times to Orzell were the attitudes of his own community. North decided he was skating on the surface of lives Orzell had insisted he get beneath. But North also noticed how he had never fully unpacked why he had become a race man, why this was the new world he had chosen. O.W., who was an educated man, could still do an easy glide into the vernacular when he wanted to make a certain point: "Heh you, whitey, hah! And ya know some who come South, they just try to escape their previous life."

Orzell worried he'd gone too far. He changed the subject: "Meanwhile, what's on your plate coming up?"

"We are photographing a town up in near the Louisiana and Arkansas border."

"You're there for pretty sunsets?"

"This is an old cotton depot place by a little river where colored folks live on the West side of town and whites on the East. You will believe me when I tell you that the Norfolk and Southern tracks run right down the middle of Main Street. Guess which side is the wrong side of the tracks? Guess where the streets are paved, and where the sanitary sewers are mostly located? And then give a try for where the proper number of fire hydrants, the new street lights, and replacement water mains can be found. We are suing."

"Well, God bless, but do you really think a federal judge is going to get into telling the city council where to locate the public privy, which streets to pave? Well you give it a try. But make sure your life insurance is paid up, though my biggest worry isn't you, it's for the safety of the folks who go to court for you. They are crazy courageous. This is an area where they not only burn barns, but houses. Maybe Faulkner got story ideas from around there. Tell me again friend, how come you are here when you had that cushy job sending the evil doers you coerced into pleading guilty to long term prison sentences? I need to hear."

Prodded by Orzell, that night North tried to follow the threads backwards. He had always pushed the subjective away; Diana once told him that lessons you learn before you know you've learned them turn into what you become. If that was true in his case, North thought the unseen learning had to do with Finian, his Irish father.

Finian had never been on a horse but for sure he'd lost a lot of money watching them. To evade questions from North's mother, he would take his son to the common riding stable near the racetrack he favored. North was never sure why the two were so close because the stable had nothing to do with betting on horses other than that the two of them would always end up at the track after the boy's ride. North knew where they were going was not to be discussed with his mother, though words cautioning him to remain silent were never uttered.

Finian was familiar with the stable owner. He told his wife that the man was a client who had to be kept happy. He'd discuss a sale of his real estate with him while the boy was out on the trail riding. North could never tell what she thought about this lame story but she never questioned it. And he didn't know much about the stable man, only that he never smiled and there was a tattooed snake on his right arm.

While North disappeared, cantering through a trail in the woods, Finian talked to the owner about politics. He thought the man was of German extraction and that was why the conversation was slightly disturbing, as if the owner, while he was no Nazi sympathizer, wasn't thrilled that it was fellow Germans the Americans were killing. He had once hoped the country would stay out of the war but he expected nothing of the sort because in America the Jews were so powerful. He complained to Finian that at least the Nazis had been fighting the communists. "You aren't Jewish?" the man asked him; Finian indicated he wasn't but then he decided to leave him to his stable chores. He took an aluminum folding chair out of the trunk of his Oldsmobile, pulled it to the fence that enclosed a paddock, leaned back with his legs on a fence bar and began to scribble in the margins of his copy of *The Racing Form.*

It was like any other ride for North with his favorite horse; he mounted the gray with white streaks on his hind quarters named Lightning—though the name had nothing to do with the animal's calm disposition. Until that day, Lightning had always been very compliant. After riding hard through trails in the nearby park that were pitted with the roots of beech and scrub pine without incident, he foolishly decided to cool the lathered animal by dismounting and giving him time to rest. North hadn't paid attention to how hard he'd ridden. In his mind he was riding like the wind, riding the way he'd seen cowboys ride in the grainy black and white movies they were showing those days in theatres on Saturday mornings in his neighborhood.

He dismounted easily enough, slipping down Lightning's soft, wet left flank. It was a mistake. When he tried to return to the saddle, he was a shade too short to make it without the granite block employed by riders in the paddock area to mount at the beginning of the ride; he put one foot in a stirrup and tried to use it as the foundation for a giant leap into the saddle, just like cowboys did it in the movies, but miscalculated, falling first against Lightning's flank, the horse hardly budging as if knowingly patient. North was just dangling, half on the stirrup, half off, when it happened.

The shrieking. The two teenage boys quick trotting past on the right, smirking, howling at him like the Indians portrayed in the same movies he'd been imitating.

Lightning bolted.

North held on until the shaking sent him down under and between Lightning's legs. His hands slipped. The next thing he knew, he was on the ground. Lightning's back hooves had scraped his chest but the horse jerked to a stop. The bridle had been yanked back.

A man steadied Lightning. He bent over to slip off the stirrup, helped North get to the saddle and led him back to the stable. The pain in his chest was so sharp it froze him; North never looked down because in a way it seemed like it wasn't there. He didn't notice the blood until they came to the paddock and saw the wild look on Finian's face. His father rose immediately; stared at the flash of red on the shirt, the man leading him on the horse, and ran forward.

Later, North could tell Finian was ashamed that his first thought was not for his son but how to explain what had happened to his wife.

The owner had come to them from nowhere. He stuck his chin toward the face of the rider who had saved him. He grabbed the man's flannel shirt at the tail as if to pull him down from his horse because he hadn't dismounted. He shouted the profanity and then a word that North had heard before and only understood part of: "What did you do, what did you do?" But then again there was this word. What was that about? Repeated as if it was very important. It would take a while before he learned.

The man who'd saved him shook off the owner and turned back to the trails. North wanted to thank him but he was gone, though before he rode off he had spit. He looked back at the stable owner, spat on the ground and was gone. Without a word. Just like on the radio, a favorite program of North's, the masked man who stood for anonymous goodness. He always saved the day from the bad guys but never claimed even the reward of recognition before he left the scene.

That was first. Maybe the foundation. And then there was the classroom visit. His inheritance from Finian.

North had tried to deny it for a long time: working as a prosecutor hardened him. He came to hate origin stories put out to justify leniency, especially the weepies. Everything supposedly decided in childhood. Baloney. Mythmaking, he decided. Oh, my mama was some kind of a smotherer or she was pinched and cold or dad was never there when it counted or just remote or demanding, took me to the woodshed, or even a bigtime harasser, or physical abuser. Then the details of cigarette burns or whipping or confinement without clothes in winter on and on, so there you go—what's next? Just fill in the blanks. Ironically, North was all for leniency because he had no faith in prison doing anything to most men but making them worse. And then, suddenly, a slow burn, and increasingly he suffered from knowing how cruel the power he and his colleagues held could be. But he still hated the stories that had to be told even if they were true—maybe more when they were true—to claim an out. Just bad novels. After a few years, he wanted to close his ears to what were often terrible tales of human misery. It brought him close to a sense of shame. He wanted to be elsewhere.

But when he needed an explanation for his own choice to leave a certain, predictable life, North went back to Finian for an origin story. As an only child he had plenty of opportunities to figure it out. It was clear that what Finian was telling him was *you can be any damn thing you want except you have to be a lawyer* and, without much thought about the whys, he ended up in a law school. There it came to him that at least in one respect his father had been far-sighted—a lawyer can be almost anything. Just like a doctor can be concerned with your bowels or your feet or your ear, nose or throat, or how those large cell tumors in your lungs are going to kill you, just so a lawyer can be a hustler or princely do-gooder or a total corporate robot or the guy who puts you in or keeps you safe from too many years in a cell. Opportunities for all sorts of transits; a cocktail of act outs waiting to be mixed. The degree or the label "lawyer" tells you little.

North never found out what kind of lawyer would have satisfied Finian because of the semi that killed both father and mother, incredibly, on the drive to his graduation. The truck driver, who wasn't scratched, had been on no-doze pills, fourteen hours on the road; he was fiddling with a Citizen's Band radio when he ended up perpendicular to the highway after smashing Finian's old Packard, a massive classic car he acquired after being bored by the Olds. "The Pack," as he called it, was no longer built, but it was reputed to be indestructible. But there was one part of Finian's lawyer life that stuck with North and helped make him his father's ghost.

North only learned the full story of Finian's pro bono life after his father's death but he always knew about its beginnings. It happened when Finian had been invited by one of North's teachers to tell the story to a high school class. After that day, he had a lot of new enemies and a few new friends. The story returned—or had it always been there, lying in wait for the right time to be remembered?—when he began to feel that a life of putting men in jail left him empty, though it took a long time to get a hold on what was missing. He only knew that he no longer liked what he'd become when he was North the Prosecutor.

Finian had told his son that out of boredom he'd put his name on the list of pro bono volunteers and he was signed up by the NAACP. The organization asked him to go to South Carolina to investigate the killing of a Negro soldier. After the end of the Second World War, there was an epidemic of Black soldier killings often ascribed to the returning soldiers believing their world would be different after they fought for their country. The rash of killings had a common element—a Black veteran failed to comply with the norms of segregation and was murdered for it.

The Association membership had soared during the years the nation was fighting fascists. Negroes insisted that because they'd fought bravely to defend the nation now they expected the government to ensure their full citizenship. Too many of their thoughts wished away Southern white resistance to claims of equality. That was certainly true of the soldier in question. He was an enlisted man from Pennsylvania or Ohio but he was stationed at a military base outside a small city not far from the state capital in Columbia.

Finian, strangely, began by telling the high school class that he was Irish and proud of it. The students sat quietly, not knowing what would come next. Then his father asked how many of them had been to Pennsylvania Station in Manhattan. A few hands went up; Finian said, "Good, good" and without further explanation launched into his tale which, he reported, began by taking a train out of Penn Station to the South. The train was slow but it finally stopped on the outskirts of Washington D.C.; there you had to wait while new cars were attached for the Negro passengers. A young couple sitting near him with an infant had to move to one of the cars for colored once the train crossed into Virginia. Finian was disturbed by this; he wondered why such treatment was still permitted. At first, none of the class commented—the teacher had told them that when the guest came they had to be welcoming—but after a pause two of the students sitting near North shared a laugh and one said something in a low voice that sounded like "So what?" His father glared at them for a moment but then continued almost as if he hadn't heard. North suddenly felt a warm flush on the back of his neck. Wished then he hadn't told the intense young teacher, just out of graduate school, about Finian's trip, the story that led the teacher to invite him.

On the evening when it happened, the Negro soldier had taken the bus from the army camp where he was stationed into the nearest town; even though he was not from a Southern state, he knew enough to go toward the rear to the colored section of the bus. But when the inside lights came on the driver noticed him, suddenly told him to move even farther back. The soldier did so but, apparently, he talked back to the driver.

One of the students who had laughed interrupted Finian, asking what the soldier had said. North could tell his father wasn't sure he should answer—holding back while talking was pretty unusual for him—but he gave the kid another sharp look and finally he told the class that the soldier had said: "You probably got out of the service by claiming you had flat feet and so were 4F."

Just then a couple of white men, also in uniform, boarded the bus; the driver ordered the Black soldier to the farthest back seat, next to a woman with a noisy baby. The soldier got up to move again but this time he shouted at the driver: "I'm wearing the same uniform. We're all out here ready to stop bullets if we have to save your..." and then Finian paused—his son knew immediately what he wouldn't say. He finished his sentence with "way of life."

"And what did the driver do?" A pigtailed girl North hadn't noticed before asked.

"Nothing, just then," Finian answered but he looked directly at girl and paused, warming to the moment, holding onto silence to make sure he got the class's full attention. Then he stunned them.

"When the soldier got off the bus at his stop from the back exit, the driver pulled over. He reached down beneath his seat and found a burlap bag of the kind in those days they used to ship feed corn. That's corn grown for animal food, kids. He took a pistol from the bag, exited the front door, and called out to the soldier who was walking away. He used a nasty word and when the Negro turned around to face him the driver pulled the trigger—shot him with two bullets in his chest. The driver calmly turned away as if nothing of importance had happened and got back on the bus. He returned the gun to the burlap bag, placed the bag under his seat and drove away. The white soldiers left the bus at the next stop and ran back to where the Black soldier lay. They tried to stop the bleeding. Somehow an ambulance was called. The soldier was taken to the closest hospital, but the driver was told he couldn't be admitted. It was only for whites. A man at the front desk directed the ambulance to a clinic on the other side of town and before it drove off a nurse climbed into the ambulance, trying to bandage his wounds. She did what she could. A doctor came out to the driveway. He ordered the nurse to take a blood sample. She objected that it would take time but did what she was told. Before the ambulance arrived at the clinic the Black soldier had bled to death."

Finian looked around the room expecting questions but the class was silent. North felt his father was ready to explode, trying to look in the eyes of every student, hoping it would result in some questions. Finally, he asked, "Are any of you curious about why the doctor ordered the nurse to take a blood sample even though the soldier was in desperate need of treatment?"

Still no one in the class responded. Finian went on: "Well I'll tell you—they wanted to know if the Negro soldier was drunk." None of students reacted; only later did North fully understand why the doctor had ordered the blood sample.

At this point the teacher, who was standing on the side of the room leaning against wall, quickly walked over to Finian and whispered something. Then he turned to the class. "Let's thank Mr. North for coming." He put his hand on North's father's back and gently eased him to the classroom door, though clearly Finian had more to say. The teacher gave the class a task to write about something shocking that they'd heard or witnessed in their own lives recently and stepped into the hall. This wasn't what he bargained for when he'd extended the invitation.

The only thing Finian said the next day about his visit to the class was a throwaway line as he was half out of the house on his way to his office. He looked back at his son and said: "It was an all-white class." And then he was gone.

Finian's work on the murder case led to an FBI investigation which in turn produced a state grand jury, also all white. Apparently concluding, despite Finian's outrage, that the driver had acted in self-defense, a grand jury refused to indict. North's father went back to his law practice. He fashioned himself a single practitioner who would take on whatever problems his clients presented; when he dealt with what he called "rights work" he did it covertly, recognizing that his wife wanted him to stay away from racial matters. As a child she lived in a Westside Manhattan rowhouse near Harlem. It had, she told North, an enclosed and grassy backyard near the Hudson River in a neighborhood then favored by Italians and Jews. With the arrival of Negroes in numbers, followed by the exodus of the whites fleeing to the suburbs and outer boroughs, her parents took flight. She felt displaced from a childhood Eden. The result was a skepticism of what she thought of as only so-called reforms. She said she felt badly for anyone who was poor but she and Finian avoided any talk about the shifting nature of his work life.

North only learned, as he was going through his father's office files to find his parents' estate documents, that Finian, during these years, had quietly authored briefs in dozens of court cases involving Jehovah's Witnesses who had been arrested while distributing religious materials or anti-conscription pamphlets. He'd written checks regularly to radical causes, most of them concerned with subsidizing insurgents in northern cities, and voter registration campaigns in the rural South. He'd contributed to the radical brother of a deeply conservative Irish mayor in an effort to block his reelection. None of these political efforts panned out at the time, but that didn't seem to have deterred him. The last check was dated a week before his death. The amounts he donated may have been small but they added up; Finian had almost nothing to pass on to North except the proceeds from the accident. The truck company's insurer conceded negligence, settling enough on North that he could eventually buy the house in Concord and finance the move south. But not having either parent made him feel rootless. He'd taken his parents for granted when they were alive. That he might miss them never occurred to him until they were gone.

North was now a man who had to work hard to feel grounded. Their death left a sting as if, because of the money, he'd thrived by standing on their grave. And he wondered if the move to the South and the work he did was a penance or a legacy.

Law on the Books
Ain't Law on the Street

The sun is slowly creeping toward the distant hills as they sit at a rickety metal table outside the moonshiner Joshua's rust encrusted trailer six miles out of Gulf City. North is holding a glass of white liquid of "the highest quality," at least that's what Joshua—seconded by Orzell—has assured him. The trailer itself is set at the edge of a grove of trash trees but it looks across a two-lane country road towards a far-off gravel pit where trucks slowly drive down a steep incline into the depths of a depression to pick up a fresh load. A huge dozer deliberately dips into the gravel pile and drops the stone deposits in the back of the trucks. The distance is too great for them to hear all but a muffled crash of the stone as it drops, but North watches daze-like as the claws of the great machine dip and raise then dip again to load the polarized rock. As the yellow painted maw arches over truck gunnels and lets go, it feels like watching television with the sound turned off.

He is called back from his trance. Orzell has brought him here for a talk or so he said on the drive from the office. North feels as if they're farther away from Gulf City than they are. Though he has been in the South for many months, mostly he has seen the clutter of the highways, a few sketchy in-town neighborhoods, and the oppressive sterility of the courthouses. He has worked twelve hours a day. Made no friends. Eats poorly. But thinking about Clem, he is as happy as he has ever been.

Orzell is a tall, heavyset, square-jawed, imposing-looking man with a gray-flecked goatee who is used to getting his way. North is also tall, but more on the thin side, as if the beer bulges in stomach and hips that so many Americans develop in midlife have been carved away with a set of very sharp, steady knife cuts. He is not used to feeling small but Orzell has a way of commanding sound and space. Now O.W. lights a cigar and holds forth. He doesn't require a preface. He sails into his topic.

"What you are going to encounter soon is young bloods who will tell you that you don't understand and can't know 'cause you don't have the key to the Black mind, the unique Negro experience. For that you just have to have lived the life. Basically, you can eat black-eyed peas and cornbread, but know your place. Still, if you want to write a check, please go right ahead."

"The part about not knowing," North asked, "to a large extent it's true, isn't it?"

"Maybe if you've been brainwashed. Such a cautious lawyer you are. 'To a *certain* extent' is what you really mean. Now, just a country lawyer myself, as politicians will say when they want to play humble, and a country boy before that—but I visited Harlem in New York City once. I was taken around by friend I went to grade school with. He played a mean cornet, worked with the Beboppers on fifty second street, but he lived uptown and tried to show me the sights when he wasn't sleeping off the high of the night before. I was just amazed. All those different-looking people, crammed into tenements, sometimes joyful, mostly angry at whitey, full of the noise of the City, using it to make music and words. A kind of art-of-life, even when it was cruel and bloody. A lot of dying young. What I took away, aside from learning that I was better off staying put here, was that, deep down, race stinks. You can't abolish it, or blind it of course, but if men were angels as one of those guys with wigs said, the only time they would be using race would be to do something to clean up the mess it has brought us. They might even the score."

"Do I hear you are talking about reparations?"

Orzell sipped whatever it was he was drinking and stroked his goatee. "I'll pass on that. We aren't here to discuss policy. Back to reality, though I'm talking too much. This won't take long if you are who I think you are, or you are what I see. If you have been one down yourself, you don't need any myths."

They both watch as a battered Ford pickup stops on the road a few feet from their table. Joshua's fourteen-year-old son, a boy called Bones, comes out of the trailer with a paper bag, he trots to the car. It's a raggedy vehicle with a young white driver and a girl in what looks like a bathing suit sitting huddled next to him. Bones stands at the open car window slowly counting the money. Then he pushes the bag into the window and abruptly turns back to the trailer.

"Of course," Orzell continues, "it's not just the Negro who thinks this way. Jews have done it for centuries—you are half Jewish, right North?—and they may think they own the special people franchise but also you'll find it in Irish Catholics—and you are also half Catholic, huh? So you know what they mean when they talk about the English occupiers. But get this—human beings, they can identify. We are capable of that. We can translate one slight to another—if folks want to do it, if maybe they were brought up that way. By the way, how come 'Christopher' if you are half Jewish? Why named after J.C. himself?"

"My parents weren't believers, but they cared a lot about religious identity. They were plainly stuck on each other, but they never resolved why they were together. I think my father insisted on my name; it might have made him feel there was Irish in me."

"And is there?"

"Orzell, I came here to be a resource, to help out. Really deep down I'm just your ordinary do-gooder. I just want to" and here North paused, finding it hard to say what came next, "be better. Prosecuting as a way of life may be socially valuable but it also can corrupt the soul. Or at least it started to be that way for me."

"Do-good, good-do. That's a hard road, my man. People make fun of it and fun of you. One thing I've learned is you can't hide whatever is deep-down driving you under a bushel basket of law. Or whiteness that isn't blackness. But even if I'm wrong..."

"Then what?"

"The do-gooder way is so boring. It's like a vision of a churchy heaven. Soft music with folks wandering around in white shifts. Marcella was raised in that milieu but she laughs at it now. 'Halla-loo, I am saved!' But understand, the wife and I, we both go to church. Regularly. Otherwise we'd feel crazy alone."

"Orzell, you are telling me to live a certain life. That isn't what I expected from you. What's going on?"

"Christopher, our people have been forever beaten, bought and sold, thingified, killed just for being us. Not even an encyclopedia of victimology could count the ways. I've read the history and it's so bad I can't keep it all in my mind. I want change but things won't change as long as you can't enter my soul and I'm unable to enter yours. When they say you can't just know they are really just defending turf. It's understandable. Lots of my brothers don't think they own more than that sliver of territory. That doesn't have to be the case. They can go conquer new worlds, but to do that our folks have to let you in, just the way you have to let them in."

"Do I hear Preachy? The O.W. who would be instructing the flock?"

"Yes, of course, that's a fact. I lecture too much but, nevertheless, mine is a necessary sermon. I'm saying don't let those race critics in, even though they are my friends. I think we all have lost the way on this."

"You think they are just as wrong as the crackers?"

"God no. But it is true both sides think they are protecting what little they believe they've got. Did I ever tell you the story of the winker? No, I'm sure I haven't. Respectable friend of mine; always wears a suit. Sitting in his parked car, downtown. A white lady walks by, thinks he has winked at her. Maybe he has. Maybe he hasn't; he strongly denies it. She goes to the police and they arrest him. Winking while Black. A new crime, huh? Craziness. Let me count the ways.

"But I should leave the racial philosophizing to the young ones. Here's the important news. Roy Scarper of the Legal Defense Fund in New York is on my back about something I bet most Northern liberals never thought about. Until recently, most Southern hospitals and medical offices either segregated or flatout rejected colored patients and doctors. There is a long list of deaths arising out of emergencies attributed to refusals of service by medical facilities and ambulance services. Some famous stories, like the deaths of singer Bessie Smith and blood scientist Charles Drew, don't check out but people believe them anyway. That tells you something.

"But in '46 we got a break. Congress passed a huge funding law to upgrade hospital construction known as the Hill-Burton Act. The driving force behind the new law was one of our own here in Alabama, Senator Lister Hill. He was a progressive supporter of President Roosevelt's New Deal; a sponsor of the Tennessee Valley Authority and the Fair Labor Standards Act. He made sure that the law funded rural areas—a choice that raised the level of care for both poor whites and poor Blacks—but to survive politically in the Deep South he had to look like a typical Southern senator. Hill inserted a 'separate but equal' clause in his bill that permitted hospitals receiving federal money to segregate or to exclude Negroes completely."

"Orzell, with 'separate but equal' provisions, the equality part was pure eyewash. I don't think they were ever enforced, nor were meant to be. Isn't that right?"

"Well, Chris I see you've done your homework. The price of political power down here is pretty clear. Hill had to hew to Alabama's white supremacy line or he was out of a cushy job. Now recently a maverick dentist named Simkins organized a group of North Carolina docs and a couple of patients in his home town of Greensboro to challenge the racist law at two hospitals receiving the federal money. He won in court and it is now the case that no medical facility that takes the funding should be able to exclude or segregate.

"Now please listen carefully because Scarper wants something from us. He says the real problems is he doesn't have the money or the people to sue hundreds of hospitals and clinics. That means if change happens it'll be up to the government to enforce federal law like the Civil Rights Act, which now says if you take public money you can't discriminate. There's a tiny bureau charged with enforcing this and they started doing what government always does— accepting empty paper assurances of nondiscrimination without any investigation as to their veracity.

"The New York lawyers told them it wouldn't do. The official first response was 'Ok, then send us some complaints'—they meant so we can cover our asses. But in just a month, Scarper gathered in over 300 complaints, from denial of service in ERs, to a patient placed in what seems to have been a closet where they kept mops, brooms and detergent, to outright exclusion, and some that seemed related to a death from non-treatment. The complaints were a game changer because they led to actual site visits and investigations. A lot of the doctors who really run these hospitals went berserk but fortunately others at least committed that they would comply with the law. The problem wasn't only refusing service or segregating patients, it was that white doctors would not allow Black doctors to get staff appointments which, of course, came with the right to admit patients. The white docs who served African American patients feared that integration meant that they'll no longer have a monopoly on admitting them to major hospitals. In short, big money was a stake.

"I'm told these white docs are not only used to denying staff privileges to colored doctors who can take business from them, but also to some white doctors who don't play golf, or socialize in the accepted way, and in certain places, of course, to Catholics and Jews. What we have is the classic case of folks who have never had to face regulation feeling they can pretty much do what they want without interference."

"Has the President gotten involved? I mean what's the politics of this?"

"A very good question. President Johnson has nudged the bureaucrats to send out hundreds of inspectors. This, plus threats that the Administration will actually cut off funds to facilities that don't comply, has led to a great deal of what looks like actual compliance. He has even gotten support from the American Medical Association, which as you probably know has a record of totally excluding Negro physicians from membership. But the critical problem Scarper sees is that ten to fifteen percent of the hospitals are only pretending they are following the law. They have all sorts of ways to hide what they're doing. He's a pretty low-key guy but he says lives are at stake. Mortality figures for lifespan and childbirth are pretty depressing. If we can show that a few major facilities are lying he thinks the scandal will lead the whole group of recalcitrant hospitals to change direction."

North had listened carefully. Waiting for the other shoe to drop, he finally interrupted. "And why did he contact you?"

"He claims the worst example of this shady dealing in the country is our very own Davis Memorial. They've told the feds they are doing right but I believe they rarely admit anyone of color unless it's for show or a mistake. They may have cooked the numbers they give Washington. Some of the holdout hospitals have done some pretty bizarre stuff like claiming the reason there were no Negro newborns in the nursery was the African American mothers only wanted to keep them in their rooms. One took down 'Colored' and 'White' restroom signs but installed locks with keys going only to white staff. There was a federal investigator who was told to visit an integrated ward for four patients. There was one white man, two colored, and one who he thought looked Mexican. They were all comatose!

"Scarper has a source in the federal bureaucracy who thinks the Director of the Hospital, Hedley Ronson, is calling the shots. He and leaders of the medial staff are working clandestinely to avoid complying with the Civil Rights Act. But we don't have proof. They've filed papers claiming compliance. At the same time, they've passed a resolution insisting doctors have an absolute right to admit their patients where ever they want.

"He wants us to find a way to learn the facts on the ground. Now, Chris, a little bird told me you know someone inside the system at Davis Memorial who might help gather evidence. If we could get some hard information, the feds would be willing to threaten the Hospital that they know all about the deceptions and take legal action. It seems pretty clear that if we expose these hard-liners in Gulf City a lot of the smaller fish may fall in line."

History Lessons

A few days later, the two lawyers were walking together three streets from the water. They couldn't see it, but North could smell it and hear its sounds. As always, the bay made its presence known. It was not a matter of just water or even floods, but of identity. Every citizen knew that there would be no Gulf City without it. Even though commerce despoiled while it empowered, once brought in slaves, and always money, disease and a supposed modernity, the bay spoke to the people as a whole—and here was an equality of sorts, as not only white people claimed it as birthright. Of course, the exporters and importers, the ship builders, the truckers and rail companies that brought in the things that went out and took in the things that were disbursed inland, and the politicians they patronized, even factions fighting over who could develop a wharf, serve on the Maritime Commission or decide whether stopping pollution of the down bay fisheries was worth serious consideration—all thought it part of their heritage.

The same was just as true of the African Americans who built the wharfs, laid the pillars that supported it, loaded and unloaded the trucks and the freighters, who often brought dinner home from muddy banks rather than from the catch of the trawlers, and the working oystermen and shrimpers who served the fish markets of the City and region. It was their bay too. Their ancestors had been shipped from Virginia and the Carolinas to the auction block where planters snapped them up to serve King Cotton. If you grew up near it or even just had an uncle whose sharecrop ended up shipped to another continent or an aunt who cleaned, cooked and nursed the spawn of white privilege whose money came from it, you knew the bay was yours because it was inside of you.

"Hear me now," Orzell observed as they headed for a shop he favored. "If you look down toward the water when we pass the next cross street, you'll see the place where during the war hundreds of white shipbuilders rioted because the company decided it had to comply with federal law by hiring a dozen colored welders. It was a bloody mess all because most of the white workers came from up country where they don't give a damn about equality. Still, it was wartime. You might have thought that would have stayed their hand. In the end, the company and the feds worked out a deal with our people where they got to work but only in teams with each other so long as they were supervised by a white foreman."

Orzell was on a mission to buy a hat, a decent fedora, because he knew he was growing bald. Marcella told him to stop looking in the mirror and just accept it. North wondered if she was concerned he was testing forbidden waters with a particular lady, a client of his in a recent divorce case, who in passing had described the lawyer to North as a "fullness."

"Listen now, Christopher. Roy Scarper must think we are the FBI. He forgets, because he went to a fancy Ivy League law school where almost every graduate goes to work for a corporate law firm, that I earn my living by making way for widows to collect their due and winning damages from drunk driving accidents and, of course, fees from representing killers, rapists and knife fighters—though they rarely pay more than spit. I've seen him argue before the Supreme Court of the United States and he does a good job. Very smooth, strutting about in his three-piece worsted suit and steel-framed spectacles. A very Black professor look, in fact. But on this business, he's like one of those pols who think what they hear in DC is what is going on in the world. Whadda they call it—the Beltway Syndrome? What's a Beltway, Chris, tell me?"

"Orzell, you're just kidding, right?"

"Of course. We don't have them down here, at least not yet, but they'll come. We are always behind because half the folks think they are living in another century. Scarper should get his ass down here from New York and help if he wants us to play detectives."

North said nothing. He had decided that Orzell was a man of opinions and that he, North, had to hold them close for a time before deciding their worth. Often this process was distracted by the enthusiasm that his partner packed into his verbal flights. The sheer joy of expression could overwhelm the content. It led to an intimacy between the two that was strong, but implicit. As a consequence, North decided he had become something different and new, a listener. He wondered why and concluded that just as Blacks could be invisible to white people, as Ralph Ellison put it in his famous novel, when race talk came around, whites often turned voiceless. Whether it was because of a deep uncertainty, a lack of knowledge or O.W.'s way of carrying the talk, North was now learning the virtues and vices of silence.

They'd reached the hat store and his partner peered at the trade in the window, featuring what he thought of as Panamas, cheaper here because of closer access to South American goods than in the rest of the country. But Orzell didn't want straw, though that seemed to go perfectly with the heat and humidity that made both men's clothing clammy and clinging on even this short walk—*on almost every walk*, North thought disparagingly. Instead, Orzell ultimately chose a high brimmed, cream white Stetson brought to him by an attractive creole woman. He moved the brim up and down in front of a huge mirror; his facial expressions going from stare to smile to frown with every adjustment of the brim as if he was auditioning for a part in a play. North could tell his partner loved the way he looked in the hat though he probably knew that the image evoked a cowboy of a different color. *Yes*, North decided, *this man is thinking about that lady.*

On the way back to the office, Orzell was even more expansive, as if with this tall hat on his head he was an even taller man. "This guy Senator Hill really interests me," he said, "because his story contains the fullness of Southern craziness. To start out he is responsible for the greatest advance in our health care history; changes we really needed. Not because he found a cure for cancer but because he worked out a way to funnel millions of federal dollars to improve the quality of hospital treatment through the country. In the South, because we're so poor, we needed it most. On the surface, you might think he just arranged for more bricks and mortar and, while a lot was built, the money was only granted if raised standards of care were promised. To get the dough, the states for the first time had to engage in serious regulation as well as targeting most of the money toward underserved, mostly rural places. With this law, Hill brought medicine to millions who never had it. Tuberculosis, for example, used to take a lot of folks away down here; these days you don't see that at all. Without him, it just wouldn't have happened—but the real history is missing without counting in his father. I don't think Hill would have become the advocate he was and is, because he still is a senator, if it wasn't for family history. You probably don't know but his father was one of the great celebrity doctors of his generation. Down here, the story is legend."

North allowed that he knew nothing about it. As they walked, Orzell continued.

"In 1902, Luther Hill—that's the father—was asked to treat a kid named Henry Myrick, a thirteen-year-old Black boy. In a fracas, the kid had been stabbed in the heart. He was in danger of bleeding to death so Hill decided to go in and stitch up the wound, in effect repair the heart in a way that had never before been done. He drained the blood from the pericardial area around the heart and then sutured the wound with thread. The boy lived; Lister Hill's father became an international star. The senator grew up in an environment rich with evidence of medical advances. Of course, the irony is overpowering. This white doctor's fame came from treating a Black boy. The cost of Lister Hill's Senate seat, his ability to fend off claims there were Jews in his ancestry, and at the same time to advance his mostly progressive views with his constituency, he had to play the race game. If he couldn't show white Alabamians that he was a loyal segregationist, he was a goner. The pols here know that if they don't take that route the next man after their job will get it.

"And here's the zinger," Orzell stopped walking and turned toward North. "Lovely hat, isn't it?" And went on with his story. "The new law, even with its disgusting, lying 'separate-but-equal' clause, unconstitutional as heat comes in August, was good for us. It actually raised the standards of colored people's health care. It saved lives. At the same time it was shit. Tell me white man, how does that figure?"

"I'm glad to know this, Orzell, but Scarper wants us to investigate what is really going on at Davis Memorial. He wants a mole. Maybe we can make that happen. I may know a candidate."

"Of course, we are aware. She is an unusual woman. And she would know what is really going on. But be careful; very careful. You probably don't know this, Chris, but before he became a bigshot civil rights legal person, Scarper was in the army. He trained in intelligence work. He won't talk about the details but I happen to know, even though he was never more than a corporal, he was assigned to the embassy in Berlin. Now don't you think that has intel work written all over it? That's what it slyly suggests. Or maybe he has seen too many spy movies; read too many Cold War thrillers. Maybe he thinks moles where the rest of us just see the old story of the powerful doing what they always do to hold onto the steering wheel. But if you can set it up, I say go to it."

"I've got to get back to the office and get ready for a partition case. I'll bet where you come from you don't know about this hustle?"

"Tell me."

"You know how our people got some of their upcountry farms is a mystery. Their land passed through many heirs. Children often scattered as they migrated north. The primary, the guy who remained and did the farming, didn't always know about or was able to get the paperwork right to clear title. For all some farmer knows, there is a second cousin in Chicago who owns half a share of the farmland he got through inheritance twenty-five years back. Maybe never even seen the land. Maybe doesn't even know the primary is a relative who has sweated a living on the land for years; maybe the farmer doesn't even know the cousin exists.

"But the law knows he exists and there are syndicates who hire researchers to haunt assessor's offices to identify such people in the old records. When they find them, they offer a few bucks to buy their ownership shares on the cheap. That's where partition comes in. You probably know from law school that a co-owner can get the property valued for sale and then work out a way to sell the whole farm if there is no opportunity or agreement to physically divide the land."

"I can see what comes next."

"Yassir, a corporation owned by whites in Houston or Atlanta or even somewhere up where you come from, suddenly owns a share of the land at a bargain price. What they do with it is threaten a sale or work out a nifty deal for them with the farmer who has no real choice. If the land is sold, our dispossessed farmer, well, he moves to the City, gets a job if he is lucky, and you bet a different way of life for his wife and kids. And just, to close the circle, it's those kids that worry me most. They only know country life; they come to the City and feel lost. What happens to them in the hood can be really bad."

"Your law stories, Orzell, are always the best, but on this whole walk something else has been on your mind. Tell?"

"It's not very complicated. I already said it. Tell her to be careful, very careful."

A Knot Tightens

North and Clem had returned to Gulf City from the Alabama-Georgia bordertown in separate cars to separate lives. For the next two weeks there was no contact as they both dove back into work lives that consumed them. North went to court in Florida to argue that a prison warden violated an inmate's free speech rights when he banned receipt of two Black-oriented publications, *Ebony* and *JET* magazines. When he returned to the office, Orzell told him they had too many cases. He was hiring a recent graduate from Yale Law School who would arrive in the Fall. "Must be on the crazy side," he quipped, "to come to us when they are offering him 150 grand at some big firm in Washington."

Clem saw her patients at Davis Memorial two days a week and at her private office three days. Evenings she went to bed early. A salad was usually all she had for dinner. Lunch at the hospital cafeteria or a takeout sandwich. Saturdays she did paperwork. Sundays she slept as late as she could at the house she shared with her stepfather. Her mother had been moved to a nursing home. She went to church at eleven. Accepting how little religion had come to matter to her, that her attendance was pure show, she still needed to look like she cared. But she blamed herself privately for the deception.

Then she rationalized, smiling to herself—*it's for a higher God*.

When he finally called, she told North she worried they would never see each other again. "Meet me in the parking lot of the Buena Vista Cemetery. Park in the far-left corner, near the magnolias. Give me an hour to clear my calendar."

When she opened the door of his car, his eyes were closed. He jolted upright. Not sure for a moment where he was. She put a hand on top of his. He turned towards her with the message that had been pent up inside him: "Listen, you should know I'm a two-time loser. My marriages just didn't work out. I take responsibility but the truth is I'm still trying to figure out why."

She listened carefully but gave a short laugh and shrugged and smiled. She finally said something he would always remember, "All lives are jagged." But she changed the subject, asking about his son and why he had left Boston so suddenly.

"Your boy? Wynne is his name?"

"I visited him a few weeks ago. He asked a lot of questions about my life in the South. We went to lunch at a popular place near the University that featured murals based on the movie *Casablanca*. To my surprise, Wynne had never eaten there before. He was enchanted by walls covered with images from the film, especially vivid paintings of Humphrey Bogart and Ingrid Bergman, but he was hazy about the movie. He thought he'd seen it but wasn't sure. I pointed out that the theatre next to the restaurant revived it regularly. Seeing it there was a ritual for many Harvard students.

"He told me he'd been taking a college course on the Supreme Court. 'Now it isn't a real intense course,' he said, 'because it's undergrad, not law school,' but as a consequence he'd looked up some of the cases that I'd handled. This was a different son than I remembered. He even ordered a plate of grilled salmon and couscous on the side instead of what I half expected—a burger and fries. He finally came out with it. He'd decided to apply to law school. I made sure I was supportive; ran through the ups and downs of law study. I felt Wynne listened attentively. As we parted outside the restaurant, I put my arm around his shoulder and gave him what I think was my most important piece of advice—that law school is painful but afterwards, when you get to be there for people who need you, it can be fun. When you're helping others, you tend to feel good about yourself. I'm not sure I could have said that a few years ago.

"I felt like a real father, maybe for the first time."

There was a long silence. "Look," North said, "you'll laugh at me. You'll say it's premature but I want to be with you. I want us to leave here—at least for a time—even though I doubt you'll do it. In fact, it's probably a nonstarter but I wanted you to know the thought was there."

"How about you? Would you just cut your ties and go?"

It was North's turn for a soft laugh. "Can't imagine it but that doesn't mean the thought isn't there. I had to tell you, have to ask if you'd do it. I know I sound like a fool but I'm stuck. Despite the few times we've been alone together, free of the demands of the benign dictatorship of our work, we are as close and as reciprocal in our feelings as I believe as I could hope for. Tell I'm wrong and I'll go away quietly."

She felt blood rushing to her head and for a moment worried she'd be dizzy. "No," she finally said, griping his hand more tightly, "you are far from wrong. I feel the same way but do understand our dedication to the work we do isn't just a job description. It acts as intimacy and balance. It's how we know each other; a kind of glue. Putting aside the obligations we both have to something larger than ourselves, how can we leave the place where we are joined at the hip?"

"You're saying we'd be different with each other. We only know each other in this particular world we both inhabit. That is how you know me. How I see you. It's a scary thought but we have to stay doing what we do and being how we are to see where it goes. I think I'd love you in the same way somewhere else but right now you can't leave and I can't leave."

Clem pulled him to her for a kiss but even as their lips met she wondered if she could *ever* leave.

They drove to a bayside park. Found a trail and walked in silence. There was a bench near water. A colony of ducks nearby. A mother herding her ducklings away from an oily smear. That was when North told her what Scarper needed. What Washington wanted. He hoped she would say no but as soon as he presented it, he realized she would accept. He was flabbergasted that he had been the one who made it happen and wished he hadn't. His first impulse was immediately protective. "But are you sure?" He challenged her as if the possibility had been broached by someone else. "Is it too dangerous? Is it not really your responsibility?" But the words only dribbled out and the flow slowed to close to nothingness after he saw the look of incredulity on her face, a look that wordlessly said *why did you bring it to me if that's the way you feel?*

The moment of doubt slipped by. She asked for the details and once she had them and heard the steps she would have to take, she told him it was almost like she was back in the military. Then, so quickly it took North's breath away, she was no longer his Clem but Doctor Clem saying firmly what he remembered, would always remember: "Listen, you do what you do in your work and you fear I'm different. Female is different? Where were you when I was in Italy? Did you make it out of basic training at Fort Dix? Ah, men," she exclaimed and then leaned in to kiss him this time on the cheek. "I've got patients to see."

Later, he found a phonebooth at an out-of-the-way post office. Dialed Sal Ferritti's office number and left a message with his secretary that Christopher North would call him at home that evening. He spent the rest of the day trying to reach Clem. When she called back, they agreed to meet at the bar of the downtown Hilton. She arrived late, looking frazzled, refusing to complain but tight lipped. After the first drink, she finally admitted to a hard day. Two patient breast cancer diagnoses in one afternoon was almost too much to bear. He moved to her side of the table rubbed her back, nibbled an ear, and told her he would talk to his man in D.C. She suddenly seemed more alert, as if the role that stood before her had its own energy. And sent it back to her.

A week later, Ronson called a staff meeting to discuss how they would deal with the forced race mixing that they were confronted with. He called on several senior men, each of whom, in tones varying from anger to resentment to regret, decided that none of the doctors at the meeting should admit colored patients to Davis, except in special circumstances. A few should be taken to send the federal bloodhounds off the scent and that was ok. Confuse the feds and make it look like they were treating all comers but also hoist the flag of sacred doctor patient decision making. To Clem's surprise, there were several doctors who objected but said they would reluctantly comply. "Ronson pointed out," as she explained one morning over coffee to North, "the usual government rules about forcing colored patients on us didn't apply to emergency admits. He got this big grin on his face adding, 'And you know we have a lot of emergencies here in Gulf City.' Everyone laughed. There were victory whoops." She had to sit through this. Not say a word. Clem wasn't sure what her face had betrayed.

The Tape

O
n the days she came to the office, usually mornings twice a week, Orzell's wife would lighten things up. Marcella was a large woman but she moved like a dancer, as if as a reminder that for most of her life she had been slender. She was given to bright-colored, flower-patterned dresses. Her tiny desk sat next to a metal filing cabinet outside her husband's office. She typed his legal papers on an old Remington machine; the only other thing on the desk aside from a picture of her son, Billy, who was in the military stationed in Germany, was a bottle of blue nail polish. She also sent out bills and kept track of payments, working with speed that suggested that she had other more important things to do, that she spent time in the office only as a favor to her husband. North noticed that Orzell smiled more when Marcella was in the vicinity. Instead of dashing out at noon the way she usually did, this day she stood in the doorway of North's work room, clutching a small package, pulling on a cigarette, and not speaking but looking down at the white man who had unexpectedly become a presence in her life.

North offered her a chair but Marcella just stood staring at him, looking like she was debating whether to speak, until she needed to deal with the butt. Then she took the only chair, patting down her skirt, her cheeks rising in her inviting smile. She handed over the package. "It's addressed to O.W. from Roy Scarper, but he's upstate on some case and told me it was really meant for you. It's an interview with a lawyer who works for the government. He says you'll understand. But I just want to say a few things to you for myself if you are going to become a fixture around here. First, my husband is not perfect, but he is a good man, a hard-working man he is. If he plays around the way most men do, he keeps it from me and that is the way I like it. If he didn't, he would be missing a testicle or two.

"Secondly, all you really know about me is that I've cooked you a nice fish dinner or two and that I went to school out of state, in Detroit actually. I don't know why I told you that my life changed when I stopped using hair relaxers with those awful smelly chemicals and went natural but if I went into that I must like you. Just so you are fully informed, I have a master's degree in sociology but I've never been able to get a job down here. I'm not sure why but it may have something to do with my husband's reputation as a man who can't be bought. Or that I'm a woman. And I do suppose race might have a tiny wee bit to do with it also. I take note of all this but deep down it is not a problem for me. Though I'm not much for God stuff, I do a lot at my church. And I like my life."

After this she paused. North hadn't said a word. But he looked at her, waiting.

"Here's my point. My teachers at the University knew more about white society than Black and they taught me that there were whites and whites; that actually their attitudes toward each other were more interesting than the way they looked at us. I mean we were taken for granted, our place was settled. They were afraid, yes, the way those at the top are always afraid that those at the bottom are resentful. Anyway, the same thing is true of our community. There's tweedle dee and tweedle dum on both. Our house may have been bombed by people we know. They may think O.W. is too, I don't know, interested in negotiating. Or isn't angry enough."

"Marcella, that would be so sad if it's true. You know, where I come from, I think Blacks and whites don't really know each other. Here the races may know each other too well."

"I think it's good to be reminded how often relationships are mysteriously complicated. The other whites, the rural ones, the 'pea-pickers,' they call them down here. Bet you never heard of that word; in the rest of the country they are 'rednecks.' The people you are often dealing with, the ones with the power to change things or to resist, they hate them more than they hate us. But they use them. To the big shots we are like children—they think most of us either need tough love to get straight or, because we're so dumb, just to be looked after. This is just my opinion. Their real disdain is reserved for the common people they manipulate."

"Marcella," North interjected, "I love listening to you. I know you have more to say but can we do it down the street at the BBQ, have a drink, and lunch on me?"

"Sorry, I'm much too busy for a sitdown lunch. But someday. Orzell probably won't tell you but every week or so we get a nasty threat. Now they're sending dead rodents in gift-looking boxes. I have an appointment with a hardware store guy who promises me he can surround our house with enough powerful lighting to make anyone with bad intent think twice before getting too close. Also, I have a medical appointment. I find it so curious that the nice white doctor who treats my diabetes talks to me like he thinks he knows everything I'm thinking. A nice young fella with superb Ivy League training but last time I looked he doesn't have a degree in mind reading. What I'm saying to you is discrimination takes many forms; some are obvious but others are very hard to see. So, there you have it. I'm off. Anyway, you have to listen to the tape."

North sat for a while pondering his conversation—mostly his listening—with Marcella. *What a different life I'm living,* he thought. *How can I ever go back?* Finally, he roused himself to find a tape player in Orzell's office. He unwrapped the cassette, leaned back in his chair and closed his eyes.

"Can I record this, Jenny?"

"Go ahead, Mr. Scarper but I'd like a copy. You understand this is all irregular. I shouldn't be doing talking to you but I'm fed up."

"Of course. I do understand. We'll keep it confidential. Now you and Megan Stewart are legal staff at the government office that is supposed to ensure hospitals comply with the civil rights laws?"

"Correct, but I want to explain it was a certain kind of law we are dealing with. We don't go to court. We are using law for leverage. Of course, a lawyer has to go to law school but I always thought they should be training us differently. We should have gone to a fact school. We get these words called laws. They're really just marks on paper until you have a situation. My government job is not only to know the words but let them breath. Let them mean something in people's lives.

"From the start I was supposed to make sure the hospitals in the South stopped exploiting colored people—stopped refusing to serve or separating them, stashing them in basements and rooms like closet. Sending ambulances away. Refusing to let them be doctors or nurses. It's disgusting. And it violated the law but all this is also very un-Christian, which is important to me."

"How did you get this responsibility?"

"Well, frankly, before I was asked to take this on I was doing crap. My boss in the office where I worked never gave me anything interesting to do. At the time I didn't have any idea why but now I've learned more. I'm pretty sure it was a woman thing. But then I was dull to it, I guess because I grew up with a feisty mom who all her life worked. She was a buyer for the housewares department at Macy's. Probably made more money than my dad. So, I wasn't plugged into the problems of being a woman in a serious job situation. Maybe my boss thought I was taking up space for a man. And in those days, a law school professor might schedule a lady's day when the few of us in the class could be called upon to answer the professor's questions."

"I'll bet none of the men in your class complained about this."

"No, of course not. I will say, however, that none of my classmates ever made light of my professionalism. Maybe I was just lucky."

"Back to the job you ended up with."

"Yeah. As soon as I started the assignment, we tackled three state segregated hospital systems where they put whites and Blacks in different mental institutions. In one state a judge ordered the places to integrate but the people in charge tried to keep Jim Crow, even though the Negro places were, well, they called them 'snake pits.' Not that the white institutions were pleasant places to be. Most of the patients there were poor; many had been more or less abandoned by their families. If there was integration, the governor threatened to close both institutions. He said if anyone tried to move the patients for integration, he'd order the state police to return them to a segregated setting. When I went on site visits to investigate, the bosses of the institutions said to me 'We are just doing freedom of choice. We will tell the doctors they can integrate or not. Up to them. We will declare that as an institution we are not for segregation but then it will be up to the patient's wishes. Can you imagine giving psychotics a choice of their roommates?'"

"How did it turn out?"

"Ironically, for financial reasons, they had to close the colored psychiatric facility. The patients were moved to the white institution but kept far apart. Things got a little better, I guess, after the change. But in the one I knew best they only had a single psychiatrist. He was a foreigner, a Cuban, with very spotty English but he was an intelligent man and tried hard to do the right thing for patients. The physical plant stunk but over time they started discharging most everyone, white and Black, relying on drugs and God-knows-what. Then I was assigned to inspect the regular hospitals. That's where the problems I saw were even worse. By the way, Mr. Scarper, how are you going to use this?"

"Jenny, let me go into that later if you will. I'll say this, I'll use it to educate our people. I'll keep it in house. But can we get on with your story? It's important for me to know if you were you ever in danger when you investigated these hospitals?"

"A lot of hostile glances and surly responses, a couple of death threat letters, which aren't pretty, but I didn't take them seriously. There was only one time when it was totally scary. I suppose you would say criminal. You know I tried to deny it ever happened even though it was traumatic."

"I think happens all the time with trauma."

"Well it was traumatic. It took place when I spent most of a day checking on this hospital in a rural county in the Northern part of Alabama. My rental had been parked in their lot for hours. My name had been in a local paper as the federal lawyer who was coming down to investigate. It was snowing when I left for the airport to get a flight home and I drove pretty slowly. Really unusual to have snow where I was, so when I decided there was something wrong I thought it was just that the car wasn't equipped with the right tires. Or it might just be slick roads. But the car started wobbling in a funny way. Steering was crazy, like what you do with bumper cars at an amusement park. The roads were pretty empty, but it got worse; finally I found an exit with an open gas station near an off-ramp. As

I pulled in, a guy, I don't know if he even worked there, started yelling that there was something wrong with my steering wheel. When the garage man put the car on a lift, he took one look at my tires and screamed a profanity. He told me most of my lug nuts were gone.

"I went ballistic and called the rental company and was so emotional—a nutty lady they must have heard—they sent a new car. You know if it hadn't been snowing, with me driving so slowly because I feared skidding, there would have been one dead federal lawyer's funeral."

"Who do you think is responsible?"

"I only have my suspicions. I reported what happened but it has never been followed up. That's one reason I'm willing to talk to you. But most of the hospitals are run by the docs. We know, for example, at Davis Memorial in Gulf City, Hedley Ronson runs the whole show. The Board of Trustees just rubber stamps whatever he proposes. You've heard of 'cash cows.' These places are not only cash cows they are—hah, this will sound funny—power and status cows. The doctors who run hospitals like Davis see the struggle over race as a power struggle. Many are racists, I guess, racists of the genteel sort, but they're also autocrats. I wasn't checking on Davis that day with the car, I was in a rural area, but you know people like Ronson in that area must have known my schedule."

"And you think that had something to do with the lug nuts?"

"Who knows? I don't have any proof. Is this ok?"

"Thanks for talking to me."

"I'll meet you again if you want but I want to check some things. I hope this has been helpful. I'm just not sure who was responsible; I may never find out. And I remind you, I'm a fact person; always just want to make sure that I have them in order. Remember I said fact school as well as law school."

Roommates 1943

From the unpublished journals of Nelson Parker

In freshman year, I went to the dean of students and asked for a different room assignment. At first, he wasn't interested in my complaint; treated me like I was just an entitled kid or even some kind of troublemaker. A balding ex-military guy, a former Marine out of the War because he'd been wounded in the Pacific, big American flag on his desk. He didn't ask for a reason. He just sat there like a rock and waited. I knew right away what I had to say wouldn't impress him much.

So, I shifted gears. I mentioned to him that they were from the East. North and Ferretti were both Eastern liberals. Because I was from Missouri, they thought, *here was a hick*. I understood that telling the dean right off that most New Yorkers had no religion— that they both never attended Chapel the way they were supposed to—would get out. I'd be looked at a certain funny way on the campus that I didn't want to deal with, so instead I mentioned the bottle of bourbon I found in the clothes closet. It was against the rules and I didn't want roommates who were drinkers.

That seemed to make sense to him, though I'm not sure if it was what I said or the intense way I said it that mattered. Finally, he told me he'd try to do it. He warned that it would take time to get me a new place, though in fact he found another dorm room for me in a week. A single too. I told North and Ferretti that I needed a single because I was having trouble studying my chemistry and I really wanted to go all out for science. They actually were really sympathetic so I wondered for a moment if I had done the right thing; in fact, when I watched their careers in the following years I was impressed by what they accomplished. But I knew I'd done the best for me because they were really tight and would never have let me in. They had a lot of shortcut references—they would talk about Broadway show music like they were professional singers. One might burst out in song, the other would join in and then they'd clap each other on the back for both knowing the words. Not my thing. That might have been meant to exclude me. I just don't know but I do know I had to get away from them because they really believed in their twosome. They were like a team. Thick as thieves. Always laughing together at silly jokes. Then there was the time that North brought a girl to the room.

North planned to be a lawyer even then—the last thing I wanted to do was to get close to a lawyer. But Ferretti was different. Basically, live and let live. Lighthearted, like an Italian in a movie. Very fastidious as a dresser and all-around neat, which was really different than the way students dressed at our school. I felt he liked me; I could have had a friend in him if he had been alone. He was pre-med, less rough around the edges than North. I had a few real conversations with him but can't remember one with North. And I think he was more principled. North had that lawyer's way of letting you know, *I'm very busy, don't waste my time.* Never could understand why these two were such close friends. I mean a doctor and a lawyer. They were always laughing about that too, even before they graduated.

Serena 1966

Serena Ferretti knew something was off about her husband before they were married. She just couldn't find a name for it and he was otherwise just what she wanted in a man. Everyone loved him for his sense of humor and a kind of gentleness that seemed stronger than what you'd expect from a young person. He was a large man, but he moved with a precision, a deftness, that made her, a petite-sized woman who often felt too small to be noticed, feel protected. Almost twenty years of loving marriage had only sealed the deal. He was attentive to her need to find work that pleased her—she had abandoned social work for a solitary and risky business making jewelry that sold, when it sold, in museum gift shops and art fairs. Despite living a doctor's crazy timeclock life, he usually made it to their son Tony's little league games and their daughter Elena's ballet and modern dance recitals. He was a devoted son to his widowed mother as she slowly drifted into a mindlessness that was strikingly at odds with a consistent physical vigor for a woman crowding her eighties. Sal even had more time to devote to her and to the family now that he had left private practice to take a government job as a member of the command structure in the health care bureaucracy.

The demands of this new job, where he could be called upon to explain policy decisions to the press or testify before Congress, had changed him. Long hours were one thing, but the faraway look of distraction was something new. One morning over breakfast she asked him to pass the cream for her coffee and he looked at her as if she had just arrived from Mars. But she still felt he was there for her and the children if they needed him. Which made it all the more difficult that she was now five years into an affair with an old friend, actually a friend of both of theirs. He was married also, but it was a turbulent relationship between husband and wife, both of them having threatened to leave the marriage but never doing it. Meanwhile Serena's marriage, on the surface at least, was, well, as peaceful as her name.

She took it up with her psychotherapist, Marian Kemeny, an older woman with a wrinkled face and gray hair pulled back in a bun who had an antique-filled office in a Bethesda mall. This was her third try finding a shrink she trusted. The first two were both men; once they heard that she was there to work out why she had a lover as well as a happy marriage, she had been told categorically that she couldn't get anything out of therapy and, with one of them, even continue in therapy unless she ended the affair. Dr. Kemeny, who looked like a grandmother in a Norman Rockwell painting, took a different tack which both warmed and confused Serena.

The shock started in the first session when Marian, as Serena was told she could call her, asked pointblank how about her physical life. For a moment, Serena just thought to mention she played tennis regularly, but then it all tumbled out. Sal, she admitted, was not and had never been a very passionate lover, and as the years went by he seemed less interested in things sexual. When they made love, which wasn't often, she felt it was for him out of a sense of obligation. No, they had never talked about it; she hadn't told him her feelings. For sure it would hurt him badly. Of course, she added, he has always had important, stressful work. He took it seriously; recently he'd been complaining that telling other doctors what to do made him feel like he was a policeman. Perhaps he was just distracted.

There was a pause when Serena expected Marian to say something but the therapist was silent, her eyes fixed just above and to the right of her patient's head.

After what seemed to Serena like an eternity, she came out with it: "So was it something about sexual interest that you missed?"

"I suppose that's how I ended up with Martin. It really shouldn't be that important. I love my husband. Martin can never leave the whirlwind of his wife; I think for him it's the excitement of living in a soap opera. A new struggle every day. But my relationship with Sal is calm. That's the way I like it. Neither of us push the envelope. While Martin and I really care for each other—at least I think that's the case—I have to admit the glue *is* sex. Some people take drugs, we meet every few weeks, except in the summer when they go to California. Even though I don't really miss him during the gap, when September comes around, we are at it again. And we are discreet, you know. I'd be mortified if Sal or the kids found out. I suppose I'm guilty as charged. I guess that's why I'm here."

Marian Kemeny scribbled words she would probably never reread in her notebook but the note taking always gave her a brief moment to reflect: *Do I open things up,* she thought, *now or wait?* Finally, she told Serena she was getting an exercise, a homework assignment, for next time: "Assume you never saw your lover again, write down the complaints you'd have about your husband. We'll talk about whether you've learned anything from this next week." She closed the notebook, stood to usher Serena out the side door of her office and lit a cigarette while waiting to greet her next appointment.

The following week Serena grasped that Sal Ferretti was, as Marian put it after hearing what she had written during the week, "Sexually ambivalent." She had been married to a man who might be a homosexual or bisexual, who might not even be aware of it, or more likely had lived his life suppressing it. Maybe proving to himself that he wasn't what he feared by being a steady, committed doctor and a loyal, picture-perfect husband and father.

Serena wept. After consuming every tissue Marian offered, she settled herself. It was perfectly clear that this knowledge would stay inside her.

Ronson 1924

Ronson's father had his way with everything and everyone or at least that was what he thought and had never doubted—such was the way of his world. Of the Sheets, he would appear to show disdain. Though more with body language than words. If anyone outside the family dared to question why he had failed to speak up about Klan shenanigans, he would sidestep and change the subject. No one would call him on it. But that he believed in their inferiority, that they were trash, would be known to all his sons, and his wife and daughter, indeed to all who saw the curl of his lips when the subject came up as it did, to be truthful, only on rare occasions. If he had muttered what he thought, that the Sheets were degenerate, but necessary, no one who knew him would have been surprised.

The occasional lynchings, attended by mobs of miscreants and thrill-seekers were a rare thing of the past for his sons, but not for their father. He had come of age at a time when hooded white men gathered on starry nights in fields not far from the family land. These days, more prominent were sudden hits, often impulsive, aimed at targets of convenience perpetrated by men who rarely if ever had attended the confab of hooded figures arrayed in squares surrounding a burning cross. The rank and file no longer lusted after the rituals of old. They kept the identifying paraphernalia in the closet. Leaders would take a public stance. Doers kept to the shadows, fearful of informers and federal agents.

As a young man, Hedley Ronson had been taken as a lark with his older brother to see one of the last gatherings near their land. A lark lubricated by drink. It happened a night when Benson, the eldest, announced that he was going to Brown's Hill to watch the cross burning. He and his fraternity brothers were going to find a place in the surrounding woods to watch the proceedings. They might even send down some demon calls, yelps and moans to confound the true believers. Then skip away before they were recognized.

Benson had never been happy with his younger brother's academic achievement. He taunted Ronson: "You're too young and too soft to come."

It had the predictable effect on the teenager. Ronson piled into a car with Benson and three of his frat brothers. At first, he declined the bottle, but as they neared the overlook fear took over him and he begged a drink. Benson's friends treated him as a mascot. They picked him up when he tripped over tree roots as they followed a narrow, stone-filled trail in the dark to a place where they could watch the ceremony without being discovered. One of the frat boys, Benson's best friend Mike Colby, was oiled with drink and louder than the rest. He started singing "America the Beautiful" and "Dixie," repeating the lyrics again and again. Ronson was afraid the Sheets would hear but he was also too frightened to tell him it would be better if he kept quieter. As they crawled to the edge of the ridge to where they could see what was happening below, in the light of three spread out bonfires, Colby switched to "Danny Boy." Benson finally put his hand over his friend's mouth. He held it there until Colby gagged and tried to wriggle away. Benson, who was thick and muscular, wouldn't let go. Finally, he took his hand away; Colby, shaken, breathed as if his life depended on it. An angry Benson put his mouth within inches of Colby's and could barely contain himself. "No more, Mike, or I'll throw you over the edge."

Ronson remembered the look of fear on Colby's face. But he turned to the valley below, where in the flickering firelight he was amazed to see over a hundred Sheets, lined up like soldiers in a double line, forming a perfect square, in the center of which was a burning cross and a half dozen of what must have been the leaders. One seemed to be reading from a large book but Ronson was unable to hear anything except the crackle of the bonfires and the regular massed murmurs of assent from the assembly. The square was surrounded by another line of Sheets, set back as if to shield the inner perimeter. Three riders of white-shrouded mounts patrolled the gap.

Suddenly Colby stood and started to laugh. Benson moved to silence him but he never got there. Three Sheets were rushing up the path toward the overlook. They carried sticks and screamed curses. Chased by one of them, Ronson dashed into the woods. For some reason, the figure abandoned the chase and made for his brother. Benson fell, his head struck, but rose to dash down the trail. Colby and the others followed him, chased by the Sheets wildly swinging their clubs and shouting, laughing, cursing in pursuit. Ronson held back. He thrashed through the trees to where he found a huge rock that had no reason being where it was—a glacial erratic, as he learned many years later—and crawled behind it.

An hour later, Ronson decided he could safely return to the road at the bottom of the hill. The car was gone. He kept to the edge of the woods, hiding in the trees, until he darted out to stop a truck. The driver didn't want to pick him up but Ronson refused to move from the road. When he was dropped off at the farm, Benson came out of the shadows, grabbed him by the shoulder at the door.

"Never say a word. Never."

The Importance of
Southern History

Ronson was too young to pay attention to the series of decisions that led him to have an indifferently-regulated childhood, a freedom to roam the nearby pine wood and creeks, to disappear for hours and rarely be asked by his parents what he had been doing. On the few occasions when he was confronted, he learned a skill that would come in handy—to patch together a convincing story. But, in truth, his father had little interest in his doings. He had started lending money to neighbors who had begun to suffer when the price of cotton continued to fall and the cost of necessaries, often purchased from the Yankee world, skyrocketed. The source of the funds came from cousin Mercer, a shadowy figure to Ronson but a name that all family members could immediately supply, who had left the state to matriculate at Cornell University in New York State and never returned. Mercer was a Wall Street figure; but in need of local surrogates, he shipped enough capital to his Southern cousin to fund an informal loan business and after a few years of success urged—or perhaps ordered—Ronson's father to move his operation closer to Gulf City and to register it as a bank.

His father enjoyed going to his banker's office in a vested suit. He farmed out the loan process to young men he hired from Atlanta and spent a good deal of his time dining with local business people, attending lodge meetings and becoming a fixture at the county's most prominent country club. He told his wife numerous times in Ronson's hearing that he did not relish the social schedule or the glad-handing, but to prosper the bank required it. To his son this was an introduction to seeing his father in a different light, one that showed him slippery and opportunistic. His father was given to telling his family, "A man has to do what a man has to do, especially when the man is a man of the South"—implying one carrying the burden of Yankee oppression, especially given how the Great Depression had created a failed agricultural base and a clear need not to sink lower in the heedless hierarchy of life.

Any post-adolescent questions about his father were whisked away by his parents telling him one day that he was going to attend Princeton University, a Northern school but one with a well-known affection for things Southern. Ronson was not even aware this was an option; he would end up spending four years in what he thought of every day as *the belly of the beast*. He enjoyed the dining club culture of the school, but not the weather or the abruptness toward true relationships that signaled indelicacy, a crude understanding of tradition. But then, he understood that, having journeyed the Yankee world, he was now acceptable at any medical school he favored; it long being known that he was destined for a career in medicine.

The last thing Ronson's father said as he put him on train to New York, the summer of his arrival at Princeton, was a life map he had consciously followed—with the exception of a few dalliances with women of the North. "Keep our way with you, boy. You can do or say what you think best so long as you know the way never changes. Be proud of it, feel free to claim it, even if you meet disdain from others. It'll keep you holy to the end of your life."

Ronson 1965

Ronson was never sure whether they asked him to take over as Director because he had a gift for management or because he was no longer the surgeon he once was. Despite its early arrival, he immediately recognized the symptoms, a certain stiffness in the fingers and a preference for doing his work in a seated position. Given the broad Parkinsonian spectrum, however, these incidents were mild and remarkably lacking in the progressive features of the disease. No tremors, no confusion, and certainly no lack of speech coherence or fluidity. Still, he was not oblivious. There were a few operations where he recognized colleagues passing through—perhaps even one of his juniors—who may have raised an eyebrow or two at his technique, though nothing was ever said.

There was, of course, nurse Florence, an older woman whose was said to have high standards and attention to detail. He saw her primarily as a big bottom with oversized bosoms sticking out of her starchy white uniform. She'd been with Davis since the old days. That was well before his time, when it was little more than a glorified clinic, a place where people, they said, not always jokingly, went more to die than to receive life-saving treatment. He was sure she would have noted any change in his work. One of his first moves as Director had been to clean house, move her into a desk job where her only task was screening outpatient admission. She had resigned in protest. *Good riddance.*

Being Director was certainly a mixed bag of likes and dislikes but he was glad to be of service to a State that held close the memories of his family going back to the 1800s. This was just before the cotton gin had come along and revolutionized their prospects, when it was little more than an outpost struggling with yellow fever and upcountry hostile Indian tribes. His service was a plus, not only personally, but for the hospital, he was sure. It now stood for the best medical care in Gulf City. Indeed, with his plans for new space designed by a leading national architect and the introduction of new programs to fill it, he was certain Davis would lead the whole region with the possible exception of a large facility in Houston. That hospital was where it was in the ratings due to oil money. He might not be able to match the Texans but he would raise much more than in the past; once the major federal grant came through. He'd see to it that regional donor support would follow.

No one disputed or at least no one was willing to dispute the soundness of his vision for a nationally, even internationally recognized, Davis Memorial. No local decision of any importance dealing with the health of the citizenry would be made without consulting him, even if it concerned the funding or development of the municipal hospital where the colored population had been treated for years in a separate wing along with emergency cases of the gun shot variety and of raffish whites who had no entry connections to Davis Memorial.

Still, Ronson had to admit it was a firearm wound, treated while he was still practicing instead of administering, that led him to reconnect with Osborn Jennings. He'd seen his last patient of the day at his private office a few blocks from Davis; the receptionist had left for the night and he was picking out some journal articles to read on the plane for a trip to a medical conference in San Diego before turning out the lights when there was banging on the side door, which he used only to get to his private parking spot. At first, he didn't recognize the unshaven man in a work shirt as one of the sons of the Jennings clan that held scrub land next to the family property in the old cotton belt north of Gulf City.

Despite differences of wealth and culture, the Ronsons and the Jennings had a long and courteous history, only to be frayed once by a foolish liaison across class lines between his older sister, Eadie, and Osborn's brother, Talifero. There had been a midnight elopement, a burning fury from his father heaped on Talifero's father for permitting the marriage; even to Eadie's expungement from her entry in the family Bible, as if she hadn't been born. A long estrangement followed. Ronson had last seen his sister at his mother's funeral and that was, he thought, maybe ten years ago. But even while his father was alive, the two families reciprocated over the Ronson land. After the center of the Ronson family life moved to the City, the remaining Jennings brothers were still hired to keep the property from decay by mowing and planting alfalfa as well as looking after the old house which was, given the fetid climate of the area, subject to rot, rats and termites.

Ronson had grown up watching Osborn at chores his parents told him were the business of the Jennings family; that his job was to pursue the finer things, educational and social advantages that were only bestowed on a few. Thus, it seemed acceptable to Ronson to teach the much younger boy the art of tossing a winning set of horseshoes, suggest that the St. Louis Cardinals, with Stan The Man Musial and Red Schoendienst, might win it all this year, or carefully observe the boy's approach to mowing, drying and baling hay. They'd talked maybe a hundred times but never more than a half dozen sentences on each occasion. He knew where the Jennings lived and farmed but had never been invited to visit. Osborn wasn't given to calling him "sir" but there was no doubt that Ronson was treated almost as a superior being. A status that, of course, hardened when he became a doctor.

Ronson rarely used the upcountry property now, except for an annual Christmas visit, but for years he felt selling it would do injury to his aged mother's sense of history. And after her death, he realized that it was a link to the past that should not be disturbed. He could certainly afford to keep it.

When Ronson opened the office door that night, here was Osborn holding up another man around the waist, an older, fatter man, with pain contorting his face. Before he took in that it was in fact Osborn, Ronson was about to order the two away and slam the door, but the recognition stopped him long enough for him to hear the plea: "Doctor, Shad has been shot and I didn't know where else to go."

Ronson stepped aside as Osborn half pulled, half pushed the man into the room, where he slowly fell to the carpet, exposing the blood-stained rag stuck into a tear on the side of his trousers, obviously meant to stop bleeding, but plainly not working. Any aggravation that Ronson felt at the shock of their arrival melted away. He knew what he had to do; and felt a certain pleasure in doing it. In being called to his art by human need. Ronson was a man who knew how to command. It was his pride.

Ronson told Osborn Jennings to place a knee against Shad's hip immediately and to lean into the wound while he went to his storage closet for gauze and a decontaminant. He paused at the closet door searching for a tourniquet. He found none, thinking as he still searched that there was no reason one would be in his office supply closet, but there was some packing paper and a roll of adhesive tape that he had never seen before on a lower shelf and he took it. They widened the tear in Shad's trousers while he lay moaning on the floor, conscious but with eyes closed, breathing heavily, whining as they tightened a bandage with enough pressure to seal and clot the wound. Ronson found a cushion to wedge under the man's head and caught his own breath. Shad would need more attention, he knew, but that could wait. He was settled for now.

Ronson turned to Osborn, noting his features in detail for the first time. He had always been good looking enough, with a pleasing mop of black hair, but he had the Jennings nose, a beaklike affair that Ronson now thought would keep him from being a big hit with the ladies. He asked what had happened and was met with eyes cast aside. He went to a cabinet, brought out two glasses and a bottle of whiskey. Shad closed his eyes and soon produced a noise that reminded Ronson of a hound napping. Ronson stared at Osborn, noting a wild look on his face as if he was being pursued; then he poured them both straight shot of the spirits.

"None one of my business but what's the story?"

"Oh, we found this blackie in the wrong place. Don't mind when they have just a knife. Handle that. This one ... trouble. A gun. Shad's one lucky fuck. But we'll get 'em. Know where to find him. Boys find him. He'll be burned."

Ronson pushed the bottle toward him but Jennings shook his head. He rose and went to Shad. Laid his shoe against the man's side and pushed. "Up, old boy, up. Gotta go."

Ronson put a hand on Osborn's shoulder. "Let's get him to the Davis Emergency Room." But the minute he said it, he knew. And Osborn shook his head violently. He knew also.

"No report. Please find me a place where he can get help."

Ronson paused, to give himself time to think. Then he went to the phone, his back to Osborn Jennings, and called. After a whispered chat, he wrote on a pad. Tore off the top sheet.

He turned to Osborn, suddenly a big smile on his face. "When you get there, you are to park behind the house. And remember you owe me. And I may have work for you, Just remember."

The Switchboard 1966

In 1876, the telephone was born when Thomas Watson heard his colleague Alexander Graham Bell summon him ("...come here, I want you") over a wired instrument. Initially, the new devices were connected to each other, meaning that listening to conversations was open to all. Two years later, the first switchboards allowed private connection but required operator assistance. When direct dialing came along in 1905, local calls no longer always needed human intervention, but long-distance direct dialing wasn't available until after World War II. In the 1960s, telephone companies began replacing numbers linked to neighborhood prefixes with seven-digit numbers, a change that one highly-placed corporate executive complained led to "a general sense of alienation" but switchboard operator connectivity in organizations and businesses with multiple extensions was still the norm. Sitting at the upgraded boards, the operator, usually a woman, had keys that allowed access to conversation between parties as well as plugin cords or switches to establish connections.

Ferretti swung his large frame out of the cab at the hotel entrance and handed his suitcase to a young bellhop lurking near the door. The kid wore a brown jacket with three rows of gold-colored buttons down the front that reminded Ferretti of the four-foot Johnny character who "Called for *Philip Morris*" in the cigarette company's inescapable and deadly-effective ad campaigns. At the front desk, the clerk greeted him with a "Welcome to Gulf City Sir" that sounded so Southern to Ferretti that he immediately felt his interloper, foreign status. And he doubted he was in Gulf City to do its traditions any good. He delivered his name, a reservation number, checked that he was being charged the government rate, and picked up his key.

The bellhop reappeared and handed his case to the elevator operator, who turned to Ferretti with a "Here you go, sir" flourish after he opened and locked the gate and took his passenger to his room. After the man left, Ferretti realized that he had forgotten to tip either of them.

The room was spare, like dozens of others he'd had since he joined the government. But this one had a small bowl of fruit on a table by the bed, some green bananas, a few apples and a bunch of red grapes. He dropped his suitcase and sat on the bed; found himself leaning back on the pillows, carefully keeping his shoes off the spread. He realized he was sweating. The Delta flight from Washington had been rocky. The heat of the South perhaps. No, he had to admit. It was what he had to do. He wasn't made for under-cover work. His years after joining the bureaucracy hadn't been so many but they had been intense. As an under-secretary he'd been involved all sorts of policy conflicts—but they were disagreements always veneered with a patina of politeness—even when budgets were being slashed, he had never been tasked with anything like this.

Ferretti rose and went to the bathroom. Ran the tap until the water turned hot enough to splash his face. In the mirror he saw there were bags under his eyes. His pulse, he noted, was a shade faster than usual. He remembered what North had said before they left a restaurant in D.C. after a recent lunch: "The City is almost half Negro but you may not see many where you're going." And the taxi driver, the boy with the suitcase, the desk clerk, and the elevator guy were all white. Before his family had moved East, his early years had been spent on Chicago's Northside, far from the African American Southside enclaves, later he'd gone to medical school in Evanston, so he knew how, despite the census numbers, you could feel you were in an all-white world. But still the absence of visible Black faces in this Southern city in this very Southern state surprised him. But what surprised him more was the recognition that if North hadn't remarked on it he might not have noticed. As a child his father had taken him to Chicago Bears football games at Soldier Field. There was a hot dog seller at a concession stand everyone called Happy John for his huge smile. He showed a mouth of gold teeth. But had he ever seen a Negro in the stands? He didn't think so. But maybe he was wrong because he had never looked.

Back on the bed, Ferretti closed his eyes and dozed off. When he awoke he wondered how he had kicked off his shoes. He looked at his watch and realized the call had to be made even if he wished it wasn't so. He checked the notes furnished by Megan Stewart, one of the civil rights people in the Department. He unpacked his toilet kit and brushed his teeth. Threw cold water on his face. Spent more time than usual gazing in the mirror. With a sigh, he found the phone next to the bed and dialed the number he'd been given but he was not connected. He tried again with the same result. Ok, he thought, the system here must require getting the number through an outside line, probably dial a nine. That didn't work either.

He was annoyed. Maybe his staff had given him a wrong number. He found the bathroom again, grimaced at the wrinkled face that stared back at him. He returned to the phone and dialed the front desk, asking the switchboard operator to place the call. Seconds later he heard Doctor Clem's voice for the first and last time.

Megan Stewart

"There were only three of us who knew, Jenny, me and an older man who left us for another assignment shortly after this happened. We were all shocked when Ferretti briefed us but all we could do was hold our breath. He was too high in the hierarchy to go on the usual compliance investigation. This one was special. He was supposed to tell the Davis people to do the right thing or we would have to cut them off. The grant application they had pending for a skyscraper-like annex would be rejected. We were sorry about the tongue lashing we would get from the Governor—Wallace had called the threat to cut off funds immoral—and their two Senators and maybe even from the leaders of the American Medical Association. The AMA saying, so far privately, that we were dumping on the doctors the decision about how to treat their patients. But it had to be done; at least threatened.

"'You have to repeat again and again,' we had trained him to say, 'that we are *so* regretful there will be a hold up on funding the modern new wing and the plan to bring in state-of-the-art specialty services. We know it's the pride and joy of the entire staff, especially esteemed Dr. Ronson. We know it's good for the community. But, alas, our hands are tied. A shame really but that's how it is.'

At the time, the White House was willing to go along with this hard line, though political pressure against it was growing. The argument ran you that couldn't cut money hospitals desperately needed. Too drastic for the voters maybe, but all we could do under the law was take away the dough. There was no intermediate sanction. All or nothing. We knew that with an election coming up, if we were going to get this done, it had to be now. So, we set up Davis Memorial as the test case that would show the entitled doctors everywhere, the doctors who really run the show, who basically thought they were immune, that they couldn't get away with playing us for suckers. The mole had passed on their emergency admission strategy. She had even named names of those who she called 'Negrophobes.'

"Because Davis Memorial wasn't yet certified as in compliance with federal law, it could only receive funding from us under the new Medicare program for emergency admissions. She let us know that suddenly all patients over a certain age would be called 'emergencies.' While pretending they were obeying the law, the Davis people were still transferring most of the few Negro patients they admitted to shore up statistics to a second-class Gulf City facility. This was, at bottom, a clash between equal treatment and professional control with the health of Negro patients at stake, but I felt we had the law and the facts on our side—the fact being that there was no way a sick person in the South, or most places for that matter, was going to tell their doctor, be they he or she, white or Black, or a recent arrival from another planet, that they demanded to be admitted to an integrated setting in a particular hospital. In general, the sick defer to their doctors and wisely so but, more importantly, the fear of retaliation was just too great. By the way, there were several peer-reviewed research papers we discovered that found the health of white patients wasn't going to suffer just because a hospital had abandoned Jim Crow.

"We sent Ferretti off thinking that for once government was going to stand on principle even when faced with the hostility of powerful people. At any rate, the fact is that Sal Ferretti delivered that message at the first meeting with Ronson and his team. He was upbeat, called us to say he'd got through to them. At the meeting they talked about how they were considering an application by a Negro doctor, an anesthesiologist. Dr. Sal complimented them on that but, so he told us, he pointed out they hadn't contacted nursing schools to tell them they were interested in hiring colored nurses. He had statistics on the number of Davis patient admits from the mole. Of over 5,000 recent admissions there had been twenty-two Negroes. They were shocked that Ferretti had these numbers. It caught them off guard; for a moment he thought the meeting would turn angry.

"But then Ronson seemed to acknowledge they had a problem and said he was going to deal with it aggressively. He told Dr. Sal, 'We are really on the same page.' But he also made clear they had to get a compliance ruling; the hold up on their funding application for the new wing needed to be removed. Contracts were outstanding; matching fund commitments might expire. And because of the federal action, especially if it went to the Medicare program, they were likely to lose patients to other hospitals in the region even though everyone in Gulf City knew they were the best hospital in the area. He pulled out all the stops. They would do what they had to do to satisfy the law."

"Of course, it was all bull. We knew their strategy upside down from Dr. Clem.

"Still Ferretti was pleased. He assumed it was a breakthrough. At the end of the meeting, he said, the room was full of pleasantries.

They understood that the money wasn't going to be approved and the pressure from Washington wasn't going to stop unless they made changes. For the third time, they offered him brewed coffee.

"But the next day, when he met with the same cast of characters plus the executive committee of the board of trustees, the mood was not the same. He felt something nasty in the air. There was a total lack of eye contact. One of the trustees, a Gulf City banker, told a long pointless story, the gist of which was that his maid Junai was a nice person but she didn't always come on time or do a good job dusting his books. The very Italian Dr. Sal even believed the coffee on the second day tasted watered down. 'Like hot piss' is what he actually said.

"Ronson asked one of his surgeons, a guy named Max Buckeley, who lived out of town, to drive him to the airport. He was actually one of the Negrophobes on the mole's list. On the way, Buckeley told Ferretti he wasn't against Black people, he loved their music, but he'd never let one near his daughters. According to Dr. Sal, he actually said, 'Even though some are my best friends.' Can you believe it? Our man thought he was getting the full treatment.

"In the debriefing, Ferretti told us how he'd had a great talk with Dr. Clem. She'd told him the backgrounds of the players. Who the haters were. Who were indifferent but would, of course, go along with the status quo, especially if Ronson told them to hold the line. Others would do anything to get money for the new wing and payments from the just announced federal insurance programs for the aged and poor. She laid out some of the deceptive tactics they'd used in the past including some weird ones that we'd briefed him on before, like the one mentioned about all senior citizen admissions being labeled emergencies.

"Ferretti said she had numbers to back up her portrait of wrongdoing. He kept repeating how shocked he was of this behavior from professionals. We were listening to this and I have to say moderately happy, optimistic I guess, despite his description of the unpleasant second meeting. Then all of a sudden he started talking about how he didn't much like being in a hotel that looked so segregated. The room wasn't luxurious but there was a bowl of fruit greeting him and so forth. I guess I was zoning out from this sort of talk and wondering where he was going with it. He kept on, telling us all about how he'd been so tired from the plane trip that right away he lay down on a really comfortable bed and took a little nap. When he awoke he tried to call the Dr. Clem but had trouble getting connected but he finally he got the hotel operator to place the call. They got her on the phone and they had a great conversation. She was all over the issues. 'A very impressive woman,' he said.

"At that point, it was like a shot of adrenalin. I came back to reality. I looked at my colleagues and they were staring down at the carpet. I saw my intern, who was also in the room, close his eyes as if in pain. It dawned on us all that Dr. Ferretti might have risked compromising Clem's identity. He'd been told to be careful contacting her but maybe we weren't forceful enough. I don't know.

"But when two weeks later it happened, when we heard about her death, I was devastated.

"A month after that, Ferretti came to my office, which was rare. In government, just like private industry, you are supposed to go to the superior's office. The higher-ups don't come to you unless they want something. And it was an unannounced visit. He started by saying that 'between you and me, Megan' he'd been having some turbulent issues at home and maybe he wasn't on his best game down there. So, he wanted me to read his written report—which was pretty much what he'd told us the day after he got back from Gulf City. He wanted my opinion, he said, about whether he'd covered everything. But he didn't include anything in the report about his contact with Dr. Clem. It was obvious that he wanted me to say that the report, despite that omission, was just fine. I wasn't supposed to suggest he tell about talking to her through a switchboard and then, of course, it could be forgotten. Of course, that was unspoken, but if you work long enough in a government organization or a corporation the message screams at you—*I'm covering up.*

"I am ashamed that I just sat there and listened. I did a lot of nodding as I turned the pages of the report but my mind was elsewhere. The truth is I did what I always do when I'm feeling crazy. I began to plan in my mind how I would redecorate my living room. Can you imagine I was thinking about the kind of fabric I'd get for recovering my seedy couch and how much it would cost by the yard? But I tried to look like I was paying close attention and kept nodding so he might have thought I agreed with everything he said. But I just wanted him to go. I was feeling sick.

"But then I was saved by the intern. I'd passed the report to him. This kid was just out of law school; it wasn't one of the Ivy Leagues schools. I think it was in Brooklyn, where he was from. His intern training agenda was for him to follow me around and for me to read and critique anything he wrote. He was also to sit in on my meetings. I liked him but we were very different. I tend to hold onto my thoughts for a while before I speak. In truth, I'm a retentive type. But this young man, well, he had different boundaries. He would speak first and think next. I didn't much like this about him but, hell, he was young. Lawyers are trained to be cautious. Not loose-lipped. And even more when you are a government lawyer; it's doubled. You can't go spouting your opinions, for example, if it'll cause someone to think that they are Administration policy. But the young man leans forward in his chair and looks at Sal Ferretti a certain way, and this reminds me he is also Italian. Heh, maybe that had something to do with what happened next because he just blurts out, 'Sir, what about the dead doctor?' His exact words. I stopped thinking about fabrics. Paid attention.

"Ferretti glared at him but then, with a pained expression, he looked at me. For him, the intern didn't exist; he was just a piece of furniture. He said, 'Thanks for your help on this, Megan' and he collected the papers that were in front of him and left. I don't think I ever met with him after that. I mean he never came to my office again or called and I was never asked to come to him.

"The horrible news came three months later. I can't remember who told me—the Surgeon General's administrative assistant maybe, or the numbers guy in the agency who tracked the formal list of the hospital construction and research projects cleared for funding—but when I informed my team, they were incredulous. Despite her death, Ferretti's visit, and the record of evasions and stonewalling displayed at Davis Memorial, three months later the hospital had been totally cleared. A letter of compliance had been sent. You could see the energy leak out of my colleagues; not much work got done in the following weeks. We had a law professor in the office at that time who came under one of those short-term visitor fellowship programs. His interest was studying how the agency counsel dealt with rulemaking—I know eyes will gloss over just at the thought of that—and he had a field day collecting responses. My intern was the only one who wasn't depressed. He told the professor that what had happened justified his rebellious side. His sue-the-bastard-at-the-government-whenever side. As I said, I liked him, but his laughter and general attitude after Davis Memorial escaped got on my nerves.

"I called a friend. I can't tell you her name, even now. She worked at the White House. A college classmate. A soul sister. I always thought she should be the first Black female president, she was so talented. Her job there was mostly policy research; way below what she was capable of. I asked her to look into it and let me know who had made the decision and why. I figured it had come down from on high and was a cave-in, because of politics with an election coming, but when she reported back it was a totally different story. She said her sources denied the White House had anything to do with the decision. The President's advisors had just gone along with the recommendation from the leadership in my own shop. She told me they said something she couldn't understand and couldn't get elaborated: the two staff members she had sought out and whom she trusted said they were told there was a need to protect the reputation of the Department, particularly one of the officials who was involved in enforcement. She didn't have a clue what that meant but, of course, it couldn't have been clearer to me. I thanked her. 'No need to pursue it further,' I insisted.

"As I said, I never saw Dr. Sal after our meeting about his report. I know that he left the Department some months after the Davis compliance finding. He may have returned to Johns Hopkins in Baltimore, where I think he practiced and had some medical school teaching responsibilities. Then later I heard the news that he had taken his own life. I never saw an obituary—but then I don't read the Baltimore papers. I have to admit that I associated his suicide with some guilt over what happened in Gulf City but, on reflection, I know that the snippets you get about why people kill themselves are often totally wrong. The public seems to need a cause to hang onto and folks often grasp the most obvious thing. You know the person was abused as a child or saw too much death in a war. I think that sort of thing explains my first reaction, that it was all because of the Davis Memorial screw up that maybe led to Dr. Clem's death, but it could have been anything. All I know is that Ferretti had a wife who had been a professional woman, maybe a psychologist or social worker, something like that, and a couple of kids. And he mentioned one time that there was some turbulence in the family, I think that was the words he used were, 'turbulence at home,' but frankly I thought that was just a minor way of excusing his negligence. Still, do we even know for sure whether that the phone call through the switchboard was listened to, that what was heard sealed her fate? Still despite the coroner's story that it was an accident, nobody in my office believed that to be true, and apparently nobody in Gulf City believed it either."

Nashville 1967

They met around a Formica table in a booth at a popular neighborhood breakfast place in Nashville, Tennessee, where North had gone to help a lawyer he'd met at a conference of criminal defenders. The lawyer represented a sixteen-year-old Black high school student charged with raping a Black woman three times his age and, on the same night, attempting to rape a white housewife who lived two miles away from the first woman. The state decided to go with the charge involving the Black woman even though it had less evidence of guilt to save the white women from the embarrassment of having to testify in public about a sexual assault.

As a result, the local man, who was a prominent lawyer as well as a part-time Baptist minister, observed that the ways racism affected decision making were wondrous, too many to categorize, too many to keep in your head. He'd brought his college-age son to join them while they talked shop and discussed strategy. The goal was to figure out a way to persuade the district attorney to let the boy be tried in juvenile court, where the potential sentence, if convicted, would be lighter. The problem, as explained to North, was that the youngster was as tall as a grown man, heavyset and dark-skinned.

The lawyer put it bluntly, "To a white man he looks the epitome of a dangerous grownup, a Black rapist."

Local people would stop by the table, exchange pleasantries with the lawyer-minister, and be introduced them to North as a "super lawyer colleague come to help on an important case." Many hands were shaken. In between these visits, they agreed they wouldn't be able to persuade the prosecutor, but a strategy might work to challenge the youth's identification by the female victim on the ground that the police had purposely engineered an unfair lineup. Neither of them thought this a winning argument, but aside from hoping for jury skepticism, it was all they had.

North happened to look up over the counter seats, filled with workers wearing yellow hardhats, the place smelling of cooking grease, to where a news program reporting a mysterious death of a prominent female doctor in Gulf City was playing on a black and white television raised above the counter on a shelf next to a blackboard-filled menu. His colleague was chattering away, continuing to brainstorm defense theories and searching his face for a reaction.

The son had just interrupted, asking North if had he been to a Nashville music club yet when "No, no, not her," came out of his mouth, a wailing that turned heads from the counter. He put his head in his hands as if to deny what he'd seen and heard. And then he pounded the table with both fists, dishes clattering, cups spattering liquid. He tried to stand but then crumpled to the floor as his colleague crouched next to him.

The father and son circled him with their arms, raised him up and took him toward a car. In the coolness of the day, bright sun mixing with a breeze, North straightened and stood, gently released himself from their grip. He thanked them. He thanked them again. His head cleared. He'd have to find out how—but did it matter? Clem was gone. He was lost.

North began to shake and cry as man and boy covered him with words of consolation. Again, he was hugged and held tight. *A blessing*, he thought, as grief overwhelmed him. *A blessing to be held by human flesh* but North knew, even then, that rage would come later.

McSorely 1984

*I*t *was really a very easy get*, McSorely thought. This creep had slashed his girlfriend's face. Didn't contest it; didn't even say he was sorry. But he'd been angry, he offered, because she wanted to break off. He wanted leniency and offered information.

Mac had plenty of proof so he didn't need cooperation from him but said he'd listen. Ok, the man said, but he needed to know he wouldn't be exposed. They kill him if it was let out.

"Who will kill you?" the detective asked.

There was no answer but he said he wanted a cheeseburger and a Coke.

Playing for time, McSorely guessed. *Amazing how often a cheese-burger and Coke will encourage them to talk.* He sent out and they sat across a table under yellow lights silently until an officer brought the food. The burger looked awful to the detective but it was gobbled down and then he started on the Coke. His mood changed. He started talking.

He said he knew who killed the female doctor.

McSorely asked him how he knew.

He said it was one of the Sheets. He'd fixed the man's pickup at the garage; been invited to play cards with a group of them once a week. This guy, Jennings, owed him money from an earlier game and hadn't paid. When he confronted him, Jennings told him to back off. He would pay except when he wanted to. He bragged how tough he was. He said that he'd killed and would be happy to do it again if he was angered. The mechanic told him he didn't believe him. Prove it? And that's when he tossed out that he'd killed the woman and that she deserved it.

"Let's be clear," McSorely asked, "What woman?"

"The female doctor. Jennings told me she was the one who they wanted to shut up. They fingered her and, he said, 'I took care of it. Didn't do it for money but to clear a debt so you don't have to worry, when I get the cash I'll take care of what I owe you. I always pay my debts.'"

McSorely asked him, "Who wanted her to shut up?" The man said he didn't know but, of course, Mac didn't believe him.

They both sat there. The mechanic didn't say a thing. After a while, he repeated the name of the killer. He said, "You promised to protect me." Then he asked, "Well, is that enough?"

McSorely promised they'd call it a misdemeanor if they could.

The detective had the name but it took a while before he could figure out what to do with it. If he passed it on to the DA, it was clear nothing would happen. Despite having a good guess who it was that wanted her to shut up, there just wasn't enough credible evidence to make a stink. He was on the edge of retirement. A pension in Gulf City is computed on the basis of your last salary, so why run any risk? But he couldn't let it go either.

McSorely and his wife were still angry at the Gulf City medical establishment. The way she'd been treated at Davis when they thought she had aggressive breast cancer. They put a big number on it and only later did they find out it was all wrong. McSorely had his work but the wife didn't work. Staying at home all the time made her a brooder. When he brought her the problem, she got agitated. After they discussed the choices, she came up with the idea. He could see how much better she felt when he said he'd do it. Anonymously tip off someone who will know what to do with the information. "Not very cop-like," he told her, and she smiled. Seemed very happy for the first time in a while.

"You know," she said, "deep down you are still a Jersey Boy and a Jersey Boy would probably get a big kick out of passing this on." He found an old typewriter in a store room that hadn't been used in years and put on a pair of the white gloves he used when dealing with forensic evidence. He got an envelope without any markings and mailed a copy of it off, addressed to Orzell Williams, the civil rights lawyer. A couple of days later, out of the blue, he got a shock, reading in the paper that Williams had died in a car crash. It was too late to retrieve the letter. He imagined a wife or secretary would open it and hoped whoever it was would just disregard it. He told himself they probably wouldn't understand. But he worried. After a while, nothing happened, so he hoped the problem would just go away. Still the letter might end up with someone who would do something. McSorely might never find out.

The Funeral 1984

North stood in the empty office staring blankly at items that at any other time would never command his slightest attention but now evoked the memory of his partner—the rim of a round, gold-colored glass ashtray on which Orzell would compulsively tap cigar ash, the pile of paper clips he relentlessly twisted out of shape to keep him from interrupting when listening to a difficult client's story, the dust covered manual typewriter on a window sill that was rarely used but for some reason couldn't be discarded. Orzell's favorite coffee mug, dregs still congealed like dead insects at the bottom, blaring out *Go Tigers* in large red letters. As best, North could remember "Tigers" was the nickname for the high school football team Orzell'd quarterbacked at the segregated institution he had attended so long ago that, at the time, there were still memories of lynchings in Gulf City.

When the phone rang, at first, North ignored it, but when the ringing wouldn't cease he picked up the receiver. A woman's voice announced that she was Marcella's cousin, Sisi; she was calling for her cousin because Marcella wanted North to speak at the service, two days later. She added that she had been told to tell him that "no" was not a possible answer.

North promptly put aside any concern about what he would say. He spent most of the next few days trying unsuccessfully to make sense of the lawyer's chaotic filing system. Finally, with his frustration mounting, one noontime Marcella arrived; without a word about herself or the funeral service she began to explain the basics—who owed Orzell money, which cases that North didn't handle legal filings were due, where O.W. kept personal documents, including a life insurance policy they discovered had been allowed to lapse. She made piles. Labeled them with a card on the top and, when she was satisfied that North could make some progress on his own, turned to him and began to bawl.

She accepted his embrace, but talked through her tears, and he rocked her body as if she was a child.

"The man couldn't take care of himself. Yet he was joyful because he loved the work. I don't know if he had too much to drink or if the Sheets found a way to sabotage the car. I don't trust what the cops tell us on this.

"Understand a person can't ask but a certain amount of themselves. He never got that. That's why you are here, you know. Because you are also all about the work. Otherwise you'd be doing whatever you do back where you come from. But please know that you amplified him. And that was a good. Now at the service you needn't go into any of this. Just tell some stories; maybe a good joke on him or on yourself. Be humble. The crowd will take care of you. We know how to do this better than whites because we've had some much more practice."

With that, she was gone, leaving North surrounded by unfamiliar papers and the need to come up with stories and jokes when all he wanted to do was get on a plane to somewhere else. When Clem died, he had kept his distance. He didn't know her aged mother or the dim stepfather who had found her. There was no real funeral service that he knew of; just a burial attended by a some of her doctor friends and a varied group of what he assumed were patients. He'd watched, but from the margins.

To the extent that North had an idea of what to expect at a Baptist church in Gulf City, it was what a church would look like in New England. All white clapboard, a tall spire, surrounded by at least a medium sized lawn. Of course, he was wrong. Orzell's casket lay in the well of a large, squat brick building surrounded by a parking lot located closer to a strip mall than a residential area. The lot was almost full when he arrived. If the site was plain, the mourners were not. A large family group proceeded him to the front door. From the matron to a set of cornrowed twins, they were dressed with style and obvious care. The women wore white and shades of gray; the men wore many buttoned dark suits. They walked purposively toward the entrance, and North followed behind them, but was immediately confronted by a well-dressed Black man in his thirties who acted as if he knew exactly who North was.

"Welcome, welcome," he said. "I'm usher Johnson. Please follow me." North wanted to sit near the back or at least on the side but there wasn't any possibility of not following the usher's instructions.

He was taken to a pew near the front, about ten feet from where Orzell lay. North was grateful that the casket was closed. He was soon surrounded by several middle-aged Black women, each of whom shook his hand, thanked him for coming before taking their seats, and then began to chat among themselves about topics he couldn't place with a kind of verbal shorthand that left him in the dark as to what they were discussing. He realized he had no idea what would happen next, so he took refuge in the notes he'd assembled for his eulogy. He was brought back to the present by the booming voice of the pastor, Virgil Sweeten, who he had met at a dinner, planned to introduce him to community leaders, that Marcella had cooked soon after he arrived. To North, Sweeten looked even younger than Martin Luther King Jr. but he commanded the sanctuary with a rolling talk that featured "God is Great" interjections, excerpts from a psalm, and a long panegyric about Orzell that North thought curiously abstract—as if the dead man was hardly known by his pastor even though this was not the case.

The mourners chimed in as North had expected with amens, urging the preacher on, and he responded, speaking faster, claiming the deity's presence, then assuring all that "Our demon lawyer, friend of all who needed help, especially the poor and discarded, the man we all looked to for succor, was going home. He was joining the lord in a place of honor." The choir behind the preacher then followed the last "Right ons" and "Oh God yeses" with arching voices:

Precious Lord, take my hand
Lead me on, let me stand
I'm tired, I'm weak, I'm lone
Through the storm, through the night
Lead me on to the light
Take my hand precious Lord, lead me home

North mouthed the words as the hymn swept over the congregation but also searched nearby pews. At first, he could not pick out Marcella, but then he saw the army uniform of the young man, seated ramrod straight in the front row, who must have been the son. Next to him, she was bent over, huddled, body crouching as if she was protecting herself from what was happening or perhaps hiding her effort to suppress tears.

North felt scattered. Telling himself he was a white guy who was ignorant of the customs of the church, who hadn't done the work of learning what a Black church service was like, left him feeling like a tourist. But then North went to a place he realized he'd never actually been: a consciousness of his own parents' funeral and how joyless and cold it now seemed in comparison. He thought of Clem and how he had now lost the two people who were close to him, and how he wouldn't allow himself to cry when he was on call to speak.

He stayed there, trying to see in his mind the faces of his lover and his partner; distracted as he was, he barely heard the call to the lectern. Sweeten named him "Brother Christopher North, Orzell's great friend and supporter" and the mourners sighed "Oh yeses" as he faced them. Before speaking, he sent his eyes over the hall to steady himself, even though it may have looked as if he was counting the house. Well-dressed men in their dark suits. Women with a dazzling array of clothing choices. Beautiful children looking into space. Very few teens. Not an empty seat. It took him a moment to settle to the task. He asked their pardon and for support because what he had to do was hard.

"Orzell Williams was a mountain of a man. I don't mean he was tall and strong, though he was that, as anyone who played football with him could attest, but that he was rock hard, like a granite peak in courage. He would go anywhere for justice. He could not be turned away. He..."

The mourners erupted with "Tell it" and "God's truth," so deep throated that North had to stop and take a deep breath. But he went on accepting the rhythms of the rejoinders, gaining power from them.

"He was not only strong but wise. He saw how much work had to be done and how all of us, Black and white, had to bend to it. He found a way between foolish color blindness and oppressive color controlling. For me, he saved my soul and he did it without ever mentioning it, without ever asking for thanks, as if it was the most natural and human thing to do. So, we are celebrating him. A life well lived but I have to tell you he was no God. Not perfect. He was vain when it came to his hair and that led him to spend too much money on headgear." A few laughs followed.

"He once tricked me into drinking some awful moonshine by putting it in a bottle of Wild Turkey." A lot more laughs.

"And he had awful taste in cheap cigars. But I forgive him because he made so many lives better, especially mine, but also, really most of all, because he had the good taste to marry a wonderful woman. Thanks to you all for tolerating me today. I hope, as the preacher says, O.W. goes home. He deserves it if anyone does."

North stopped there. Breathless. The mourners shouted praise back at him. He stared out at the group. He nodded. He smiled and mouthed thanks. As he began to step down from the dais, he looked out across hall and saw a man standing at the rear against a wall, staring at him directly across the great vacuum of air above the heads, above the pews. He was the only other white man present. North wasn't sure, but as best he could tell it was the Gulf City chief of detectives slowly nodding his head as he caught North's eyes.

The Letter

The usher knew he was police but not his name. He offered a seat in a back pew, but McSorely shook him off and stood against the back wall, looking, he hoped, like he was present to assure security of the service. A crowd clustered around North as he slowly made his way to leave. Parishioners thanked him, many reaching out to touch his shoulder, to shake his hand. McSorely waited them out. Finally, he fell in step with North, pointing to a beat-up black Ford sedan, the make of choice for Gulf City police, but this one was unmarked. They drove to a corner of the parking lot of a nearby shopping mall. The only words uttered were when the detective commented on the vehicle, "My old ride. Bought it used from the Department. Cost a bit for a repainting to get rid of the markings."

North turned to face him. He didn't have to wait long.

"I'm talking to you because I don't trust death. There's a letter coming to lawyer Williams. You'll want to make sure it isn't discarded because he's no longer with us."

"A letter from you?"

"Let's say it's from anonymous."

"Why the mystery? What's it about?"

"An accident that was really a murder. You'll figure it out. Now where would you like me to drop you? You have a car back at the church?"

"You're talking about Clem aren't you?"

"I'll take you back." The detective slid his right hand toward the ignition but North reached over and removed the key. McSorely made a motion to find his revolver but North angrily pushed his arm away.

"Why was this information going to O.W.? Why now me? Murders are your business."

McSorely said nothing. He opened his palm for the key. North shrugged and returned it. The detective took it and was about to start the car when he spoke to North.

"All right, you win. I can't go any farther with this. It's up to you. If I reopen the case, nothing will happen, except maybe they get rid of me. Of course, they may do that anyway. They've never been sure they could trust me; I've probably been here too long. All I have is the facts but not enough to back them up for anything like a prosecution. Even assuming I'm wrong about that, unless more evidence comes in, there's no way the district attorney will go forward. He probably wouldn't go forward even if the proof mounted up. And if I'm wrong about that too, no Gulf City grand jury will indict. They now have a few colored men who serve but that's just window dressing, you know, to look good for the federal courts."

"And this letter, it's supposed to tell who was involved, who did it?"

"It'll send you there. The letter will tell you what you need to know, but proving it is another matter. That's the problem you'll have to solve. Now where's your car?"

Death Row

North spent the months after Orzell's death avoiding what he knew must follow. He settled many of his partner's cases, doing the paperwork that authorized distributing his few assets to Marcella and their son. His first impulse was to offer the cases that still remained to a recent law graduate who was setting up shop in Gulf City and return to some version of his previous life. But with Clem and Orzell gone, he accepted that, at least for the short term, if he could pay the rent he would in some small way to try to fill the empty shoes of his partner for the people who depended on him.

His work was welcomed but he realized that changes were taking place that allowed him to free himself of this self-imposed burden. There were a few newly-minted Black lawyers coming into Gulf City, often recent graduates of highly ranked law schools as a result of efforts to diversify institutions that had previously been indifferent to inclusion of Black applicants. The new attorneys were often native sons (and one native daughter) but they also were keenly aware of what little they knew about setting up a practice or dealing with a justice system that was still dominated by Jim Crow thinking. They sought him out for advice and he responded as best he could. He also referred potential clients to help them get started.

North's income fell off, not that he needed much, but he realized a measure of financial independence by winning a settlement in a wrongful death case. An Army veteran, working as a bus driver, had been shot while he was an innocent bystander during a police raid of a Black men's club. He'd also referred a plaintiff who had died of lung cancer to a specialist in litigation against tobacco companies. When the improbably large damage award came, he received a startling finder's fee from the lawyer. His first impulse was to send the money back—he'd done no work on the case—but it would see him through to paying the costs in a number of cases where he was representing poor clients he felt were unjustly treated. He wrote a law school classmate who had sat on a state's bar association ethics committee asking what he should do. The response was terse. The lawyer replied that if the payment ultimately came from a tobacco company he was honor bound to keep it. The man added that his father, a chain smoker, had died of lung cancer. At the bottom of the letter, he'd scrawled in red ink. "Fuck 'em."

When North finally opened the letter, he saw the name Osborn Jennings, a man who had just been sentenced to death after conviction for hiring the killers who had murdered his much younger wife, who was pregnant. He was speechless.

The one prison in the State where men subject to capital punishment were housed was an hour drive Northeast of Gulf City in a rural county were the correctional institution was the major employer. When North called the prison to make certain Osborn Jennings was housed there and to find out the visiting hours, he was told that only immediate family members and attorneys of record were allowed to visit death row prisoners. The weariness of voice at the other end of the phone told him the same message had been delivered to disappointed callers hundreds of times: "Unless you can prove you are one of those or a spiritual advisor the man puts on his approved list, you are not permitted entry."

His next call was to the court appointed lawyer who represented Jennings in his murder trial. The man was a single practitioner with an answering service. Three calls to the service yielded no call back. Finally, North went to the Gulf City courthouse, found the lawyer's name on an upcoming docket list and waited outside the courtroom where the lawyer was supposed to be. When it became clear he wasn't there, North asked a bailiff if he knew him and was told he could probably be found across the Square at the Toliver's BBQ. North asked at the counter and was directed to a table in a far corner of the restaurant where four middle-aged men, all wearing white shirts and ties, were eating lunch.

As he walked toward the table, he called in a loud voice for Palamore Sykes. A short, beefy man with a napkin tucked into his shirt, partially covering red suspenders, turned towards him. The other men looked up. None looked friendly; the one man in the group who knew North from court wore a serious frown. He looked like he'd spotted a dangerous intruder. There was an empty chair at the table but no one offered it. North put on his best smile for Sykes. He tried to ignore the others and came to the point. He required a favor. He had to talk to Osborn Jennings but his lawyer card wasn't enough. He needed to be part of a visit authorized by his appointed counsel.

Sykes listened, while never looking up from the cornbread and gravy on his plate. His eyes met the other men. He turned to North: "You want access but it won't do you any good cause they don't permit conjugal visits."

The men erupted. The table itself seemed to bounce. Sykes laughed so much his coughs became fitful. North winced but stood silent as a pillar until their joy ceased.

Sykes finally raised himself and put an arm on North's shoulder, "Just a little fun. You all forgive us. Of course, lawyer to lawyer courtesy, I'll add you on the roster as a consulting attorney. But why do you want to see this bastard? He's guilty as sin; hired two guys to kill his pregnant wife. He deserves what the jury gave him."

North was stuck for an answer and he blurted out the first thing that came to him: "He has a friend I need to know better."

The men stared at him but said nothing. Sykes eased himself back in his chair. He raised a fork and turned to North: "I'll take care of it this afternoon."

North was aware that fulltime defense attorneys knew far better than a former prosecutor the overwhelming dreariness of jails and prisons. Prosecutors usually only have their imagination. Perhaps that was one reason they were free with their recommendations for longterm incarceration. But North's first supervisor was a different kind of prosecutor. He insisted that his new charges spend at least a day visiting one of places they would end up sending convicted men and women. North was sent to a federal prison on the outskirts of a depressed Western Pennsylvania town where factories that once made cigarette lighters and fabricated bumpers for the auto industry were on their last legs. A corrections officer assigned to give him a tour showed him the visitor's room with a long line of snack-filled vending machines. "We tell visitors they better bring lots of quarters because we don't make change." Called away, the officer passed North off to a trustee inmate, Isaac Jones, an elderly balding Black man with a big smile serving a long sentence for selling drugs. Jones was garrulous. He nonstop questioned North about his approach to plea bargaining, asked if he was married, and whether he treated Black defendants differently from whites.

Jones didn't always wait for an answer but while walking North through the cell area gave him a tutorial on institutional life. The food was tasteless; if you weren't careful with what you took in you'd end up with the runs and a puffy belly. They charged ridiculous prices for phone calls. Compared to other places where Jones had done time, it was at least quiet. He waved at a tattooed, muscular white man and told North the motorcycle gang guys were white racists but they kept the place peaceful. He got on with them; no trouble. Inmates sometimes were visited by a volunteer dentist, which he appreciated. You could get academic college credit with correspondence courses but there were also a few professors who came for the local community college. The place was located so far from decent transportation that there were few visitors. "It was all politics," Jones said, "the prison got put down in this rural district so some congressman could claim he brought jobs to the boonies." When North asked him when he would get out, Jones kept walking. "Actually," he replied evenly, "I'll probably die here."

The prison in Alabama where Jennings was held seemed located on another planet. Surrounded by empty fields, barbed wire topped steel fencing and concrete walls, and the town nearby was sleepy bordering on dead. The heat was unbearable. The town didn't advertise that it hosted the only place in the state where executions took place.

North showed his paperwork to a guard who sat behind a glass wall. He emptied his pockets and cleared a metal detector. He was allowed to keep his wallet but had to give up the Olympus miniature recorder he hoped might avoid detection. He gave another guard a lawyer's speech about needing it for client communication but he was told in a snarky tone that he'd be lucky if he got it back later.

He was taken to a chair in a room divided by a glass partition and waited for Jennings to arrive. When he was brought, in an officer removed his handcuffs but not leg shackles; then took a seat just outside the room. He could see but not hear. Jennings sat across from North. He leaned into a microphone: "Sykes told me you were coming. Who the fuck are you and why are you are here?"

"Don't worry who I am quite yet. Some folks predict you're headed for the Yellow Mama. I need you to tell me if you're looking forward to your last meal or if you want to join the general population, where I understand there's a crowded dormitory and no privacy; that it's noisier than hell there but you can at least look forward every day to fogging a mirror."

"Sykes told you that?"

"You know the Supreme Court tried to do away with the death penalty some years ago. That's over now. Capital punishment is back here so whether your time is up or not depends on the goodness of the state courts."

"They're not going to kill a white man."

"I wouldn't be so sure. No better way to prove the state isn't discriminating. Makes the race statistics look sweet. Let's face it, your case isn't a very attractive one for mercy. You paid guys, I understand, to kill your pregnant wife. And they did it. No serious claims of innocence. No hair samples, bite marks, or even finger prints for you to challenge."

"Sykes says he'll get my friends to contact the governor."

"Now you listen to me; I don't have all day. Listen well, because after I say what I have to say I'm out of here and you can take your chances with white Alabama Justice. I can't promise you anything but I'll do my best to see you are represented by the best death case lawyers out there. The folks who stopped the electric chair from working in this building and a lot of other buildings around this great nation of ours. Here they stopped the Yellow Mama for 18 years before executions could resume. That's 18 years you hear me? These guys are good. I know them well.

"Now one more thing. While we are talking, some states are experimenting with lethal drugs. They claim it'll make things at the end go painlessly. Maybe you are cool with going out that way if things change here, but otherwise, if they still use the electric chair, understand your flesh is likely to burn and smoke before you're totally gone. All you have to do, unless you want to take your chances with Sykes, is tell me who led you—no, I'll say *misled* you—to the other killing. I don't need the details. I need a name. I get the name and you get new lawyers."

"What other killing?"

"My friend, don't fuck with me. You hired two fools to kill your wife. They did the deed. You didn't pull the trigger but here you are on death row. Now, something very much like that happened in your life before, only that time it was you on the other end. Who paid for the bullet? Tell me, how does a woman die on her front porch with a chest wound from her own gun? Tell me that first."

"A stupid woman might come out of her house at night waving a pistol around just because she heard something. The dumb bitch might trip and the gun goes off." Jennings looked up at the ceiling. He blew his nose into the sleeve of his jumpsuit before he went on. "Course, it wouldn't take much for a person to grab her and then wrestle the gun from her. The gun goes off and she falls over. Things like that happen, don't they?"

"Someone paid you."

"No one paid me."

"You're right. My mistake. Someone made it happen. I don't know if you were doing a favor or whether you were extorted and I don't care. What I care about is who."

"You want me to rat someone out."

North pushed back his chair and stood. He motioned to the officer.

"It's been nice knowing you. I hope you avoid the bad news. I am against capital punishment, even in a case like yours that seems to call for it, for that matter, in all cases. Never have figured out how killing folks will stop folks killing but there you go."

Jennings remained seated. Motionless. But as North moved toward the door he rose, waved his arm and shouted: "No, stay here. Officer stop him. Stop him. We got more time to talk."

North took a deep breath and hoped his sweat didn't show. His fingers were fisted. He paused, waved the officer off. Took his seat and removed a small piece of note paper from his wallet and a stub pencil that had avoided detection. Ok, talk."

Comfort Acres 1985

North spent most of his time in a quiet corner of the wrap-around porch of the ornate Queen Anne-style main building with no idea where he'd settle when the weather turned. He favored a white wicker chair with a deep paisley-covered cushion. A place where the old man would always find him. There was a view of the algae covered lake. The gleaming white vans, when they came, parked out of sight near the sheds holding refuse and recycling. Always three men, always dressed in black suits, white shirts, black shoes, and ties. They pushed a gurney covered by a green plastic tarp and disappeared through a rear entrance.

North closed his eyes, better to construct the steps he imagined followed a death at the facility. Despite its costs and amenities, The Acres, as it was known, had but a small staff of foreign-trained doctors who came irregularly; they were not officially recognized by authorities to complete death certificates. A corpse would be taken via the unmarked vans to a nearby funeral home where the local doctor who held the contract would take a look, examine any documents provided by The Acres staff and sign off. He expected that the exam would be cursory; enough for the man, and it would be a man, to earn his fee and be gone.

He turned away from his view of the waiting van as a cocoa-colored woman in a red dress strode toward him with what looked like a case holding one of the new computers he'd heard about slung over her shoulder. Hair piled high, with brown ringlets. His eyes watered. *I wonder,* he thought, *how she found me.*

"Olivia, my dear, how nice of you to visit a senior citizen. I hope you've brought cookies. But why ever have you come?"

"What a warm greeting for an old friend. But as you asked, you're always on our mind. You've been out of sight recently but I don't have time for the niceties. Seems we have this very engaged professor in Philly who can't let it go. She is suggesting that what happened to Clem, who she knew, was no accident, but murder. I suspect that she might know how it happened, though she refuses to come out and say so. But maybe she heard from Clem that you two were friends of some sort and she says she now needs your help."

"What's in it for her and why does she think a retired lawyer who was a friend—of some sort as you put it—is the place to go?"

"I was just trying to be tactful but don't be cute with me, North. I just heard you'd moved into this place. I don't know anything about why you'd retire. You look pretty good to me. But listen, she doesn't trust the local cops and won't go to the FBI unless there is proof because she thinks they will file away whatever she has to say forever. These academics are always looking for a discovery they can publish."

"Well regardless, I do miss seeing you because I haven't been sassed in a few years but truly I'm a happy resident here. It's where I should be. As you can see, my surroundings don't much look like a law office. The first time we met you didn't know what to make of me. I'm not sure I knew what to make of myself back then either."

"Back in those days I'd heard from Marcella that there was this former U.S. prosecutor from Boston investigating the church burnings among the pecan fields in South Georgia and in the rural surroundings of Gulf City. You know, before you got here the Williams house was bombed, almost totally destroyed. Never clear whether it was the Klan or some locals who thought he was too much for nonviolence. I was thinking you may have been looking into who did it. I was curious.

"Anyway, Marcella said to me, 'He's white,' as if you'd be anything else. Back then maybe five Blacks in that job in the whole country. Maybe just two. You had a desk in the room where I knew Orzell kept a lot of the junk, so I wandered back to take a look. There was more smoke in the room than air. I hope you've stopped smoking. You took one look at me and said, 'Hi honey.' 'Hi honey,' can you imagine? Just another white man with an attitude. So business like! I learned to love you but I've have never forgotten the intro.'"

"But you didn't right away call me out the way I bet you would today."

"Oh, I never went to cotillions as a young person but my parents still brought up a cotillion girl. Never lose your cool. Always be polite, even with crackers. And come on, civil rightser or not, a woman like me had to be suspicious of a white man. You knew Merton Kalish?"

"Of course, but only from a distance. The whole world watched him in court. I saw him in person once before a jury. A crazy murder case. He put the prosecutor on trial, the judge on trial, the jury system, everybody and anything but the accused killer who he was representing. Now that is common stuff but he did it in a way that got noticed. The media loved him. He did do some unbelievable legal gymnastics for The Movement. Can't deny that. But he was mostly a one timer. Name in the paper. Start the case. Then move on and let someone else, conventional types like me and my friends, clean up the mess. Why bring him up?"

"Because he jumped every Black girl he could get in a corner."

"I have to admit I'd heard pretty much the same story too. You know, when we talk like this I fall for you all over again. But why didn't you see me as just another Kalish?"

"Oh, come on. North. You just think being cute is a way to get on my good side. I suppose there are those who think you are sexy but I never felt any vibrations from you were directed to me and a Black woman knows these things. Let's cut the banter. You are talking to a well married person. I have kids. And maybe, one day soon, grandkids. Flirting is out. And while you always enjoyed the attention of the female persuasion it was pretty clear where your feelings went. Do you spend a lot of your time remembering her? I have to ask, are you still in mourning?"

"She's so long gone ... but then, in a way, I am too."

"Crap."

"Doesn't sound very Black cotillion."

"Look it's up to you but to be honest I really do need you because most everyone else is gone. Maybe only you and the professor remember. And for some crazy reason, she thinks you may know if she's right about who did it."

North waved Olivia to a chair. He needed to think. She didn't believe he belonged at The Acres and she had no idea why he was there. Had no idea what he knew. She hadn't visited for herself. She was a front row player in Washington now. He put it together quickly; she'd heard he was suffering and found a remedy. He looked down the porch. The old man had started his bent walk towards them but when he saw that North was with someone, he retreated to the lobby. "You don't need me, Olivia, I know you can find others. You are trying to save me."

"If this was a movie, Christopher, I'd leave now and I am certain that in a few weeks you'd come around and beg me for the details. Your character's needs would overwhelm your doubts. You'd find me and join up. But this isn't a movie. I have things to do. Politicians to lobby. You are up-to-speed on the work I do these days and who I do it for. I'm not waiting. It's now or never."

"Olivia, isn't it foolish? Do I really want to take the past into the present?"

"Depends on whether you're hurting. I can see it coming. Next you'll be saying you're too old but I can tell you're not."

"You found me at Comfort Acres. Look around you. We have a heated pool, a dietician, a beautician, a book club, a history club, aerobics and what passes for movies. What more would a fellow want?"

"You probably also have the services of an in-house mortician."

North believed Olivia was unafraid and self-possessed. She had set up an advocacy operation in Mississippi a year after she left school, long before there were any resources on the ground to protect her. She was harassed and threatened but never in public betrayed the fear he knew she felt. She was a woman who only said what she wanted to say. He knew there was a subtext to this visit but didn't think it likely she'd admit it. But he would try: "I need my exercise. Let's take a walk around the lake before the wheelchair parade."

"I don't want to know what's happening with your body but your mind looks fine to me and that's what I want."

"You know you can always have that part of me. I'll just take the commuter train down to Gulf City and get off like Spencer Tracy in

Bad Day in Black Rock and find the killer. That way you can add to your rep as the second coming of Ida B. Wells and I can go back to chasing the widows if that's what you think?"

She ignored the jab. "There must be a lot of them in this place? I see a lack of, well, gender diversity."

"It's not as bad as you think. These days men live longer too but most of them have problems with their utilities."

"Unpack that?"

"It's a quintessential male thing. Use your imagination."

"And the women?"

"It's not quite sex but a sort of emotional cuddling they want. The men are limp, the women are dry."

"Oh, my lord. I never expected to be talking about such stuff. I just want you to find out how Clem's life ended. If you don't mind me asking, really, why are you here? Are you sick with some horrible disease that doesn't show itself to others? You aren't that old. I mean we were all basically kids in the civil rights years. We saw you as an unbelievably old white guy for what you were doing but now that I am over forty myself I see it differently. You weren't so old then and you're not now."

"They let you in at The Acres if you're over fifty and can count down from a hundred by sevens. Let's just say that for me it's a way of settling some old issues. Clearing the deck. Something like dejunking your house only doing it with your mind."

"If my mama heard you speak like that, she would say you were speaking in Choctaw. That means, *I don't understand*."

"I'm here because it's a good place to study history."

"Talking in circles. I'm having a feeling you're not talking to me straight. But if you aren't sick. I'm so glad. That was what I feared."

"Let's put it this way, Olivia, I have a few more goals to attain before I pack it in and this seemed the best place to attack them."

"My, my, sounds so mysterious. Do you have a strategic plan too? Ok, ok, needn't answer but, North, you do know why I am here?"

"Maybe belief in redemption. You can't raise the dead but you can make me feel better."

"Think of it as you wish."

North was surprised that he had a speech ready. "Well I'll appreciate any such thoughts, Olivia. I'm touched. You and your team were always a source of support in the litigating years. But look, if you are over fifty and don't have a terminal disease, they'll take you. It's big business. Once you're in they keep you even if you falter. Even if you get the bad cancer news. Even if you're on the dotty list. Just so long as you continue to pay the bills. I've managed so far. My ex-wives have chipped in."

"Ok, then if you are still healthy you can help me out with the professor. If we can find out who did it, how it really happened, I'll want to make something of it. Clem was a good friend, a brave lady, who never got her due, up there with the righteous."

North felt his eyes dampen and tried to cover it up by changing the subject. "As to your praise for how I look, that's what folks say all the time to us oldsters. When you hear the 'You look fine' too often you know that it's time to step back and accept things are about to go downhill."

"You're trying to distract me. I don't buy it but ok this could be your last chance to make things right. We have some leads. The professor says there is something fishy about how quickly the City took up with blaming the victim gossip. You know because you were there, the usual—she had an affair with a Black man, or she was a lesbian, etc. and so forth. What you might not know is what the professor told me. There is a cop, a detective, who she thinks knows something nobody else knows. A member of my staff was in Gulf City because of that killing—random we understand—of a young man in Mobile recently, and talked briefly with the cop, but he was reticent. He needs some attention from an ex-prosecutor."

"Still on the force?"

"No, I think he's retired. I've got memos for you. One is about him."

"Send 'em on but I can't change history."

"But you can feel better. So, you'll do it?"

"Olivia, are you trying out for one of those Genius Grants?"

"North, stop playing with me. Will you do it?"

"On one condition."

"Speak."

"I find him—and of course it's a him—then he ends up dead. You'll defend anyone who gets charged with it, even if it me."

"North, my dear friend, remember I'm a civil rights lawyer not..."

"You want justice, or maybe some type of fundraising type story for your NGO? What's wrong with revenge? Don't you think this guy should be burned, then hung on a tree with a sign that says 'White supremacist lived here?' Preferably across the Square from a courthouse that has one of those gunmetal gray monument rebels with an army cap and a rifle staring at the building."

"Ah, I do remember why you were always my favorite white liberal."

"I'm glad to see you, Olivia. I am grateful for your visit. I promise to keep in touch. But don't trip over the walkers and wheelchairs as you go out. Be careful."

"North, a Black woman has to be careful ... always."

The Old Man

O n his first day at Comfort Acres, North had watched him shuffle his way to the dining hall, give a quick half smile to Georgia, the hostess who shepherded "guests"—North was taken aback when the term was first used to describe him—to their tables and settled himself near a window. No one joined him. He looked up at the Black waiter who was explaining something about the menu. The waiter nodded to the old man and then disappeared though the swinging door at the end of the dining room to the kitchen. The man waited, staring straight ahead, his face expressionless. He betrayed no interest in anything other maintaining the rigidity of his gaze.

The following evening, after supper, new arrivals were briefly introduced to the guests in a room off the lobby that served as a lounge furnished with soft gray couches and puffy armchairs. At first, North thought the old man absent from what apparently was a common ritual greeting of newcomers, but he finally spied him sitting in a corner of the room. Plainly, he once had been powerfully built, muscular and sharp eyed but now he looked diminished—shrunken, bagged eyes, sunk down in one of the stuffed leather chairs North associated with private men's clubs.

When she finished the introductions Georgia, the hostess North had talked to earlier, put her arm gently on his elbow, steering him to where he had asked her to take him.

"Doctor Ronson," she began, then paused until he gave a sign of recognition, "here is a new arrival who has heard about your important work. He wants to meet you. I hope you will personally greet our new guest Mr. North. I think you two professional men would enjoy knowing each other. And kindly remember, doctor, while I never intend to intrude, I always am telling our guests that they should take meals with another. Our preference is that guests keep in contact. It's good for you."

She turned from the old man to North and with a sweep of her hand seemed to usher him forward. The doctor looked up, took him in, and then pushed a finger out in the direction of the nearest chair.

North took the chair and leaned forward to shake hands. "Pleasure, Chris North." But the doctor said nothing. His eyes set above North's left shoulder. The silence grated on North but he held his tongue. Finally, Ronson spoke: "I'm warning you. The Key Lime Pie isn't up to snuff. They don't bake it long enough; also I question the source of the lime juice—but hardly matters at our age."

North took a deep breath. *Was the man bonkers, just old, or could he be wily?*

"Not a pie guy," he said. "Prefer whiskey."

The doctor perked up and his eyes found North's.

"Now you're talking. There's a FlyBy Bourbon I used to keep around but now I'm just a wino. Miss Georgia and her ilk try to keep us away from the sauce but I have my ways."

"They're in charge of you?"

"No, no it's just soft love. This is not a medical facility. I know about such things. Fact is I'm a bigshot. They just want me to stay in good shape so they can tell applicants how upscale they are. Also, I can tell them how to assay the inmates. I'm a doctor."

"Inmates?"

"Whatever... So who are you again?"

"Just a new guy on the block."

"You look so young."

"Old enough you to pass the test. Tell me about when and how you got to be a bigshot."

"I'm pleased to meet you. People here don't always recognize me. Too many codgers. Excuse me but I have to take a piss. My prostate is a huge insult to my bladder. I know all about that too because you see I'm a doctor. See you around."

"I'm sure of that."

The Ladies

Beatrice and Susannah watched the strollers from their wheelchairs near the large window that faced the manmade lake.

They knew almost every guest at Comfort Acres, if not by name, by face. Rather than spin their chairs to the TV room of a morning, they amused themselves by keeping track of coming and goings. Bea was the romantic; Susy the skeptic. This morning, they talked of North and Ronson, though they only knew North as the "Yankee young one" and Ronson as "the Big Doctor."

"They keep company more and more," Bea said. "Isn't it sweet that the Doctor has someone to look after him?"

"Not sure," Susy replied, "What a bright fellow like that Yankee Mr. sees in the Doctor, I don't know. He is no longer calling the shots in town the way I heard he was when he ran Davis Memorial. He may have few marbles left but he keeps telling the same stories. I mean how many times? He's losing it."

"Susy do you think the Yankee has some fatal condition? I mean he looks pretty fresh to be here. Not a lot of wrinkles. Still a good-looking man. Believe me, I saw him on a bicycle the other day. So why?"

"They check you are over fifty before they take our money, Bea, so he has to be eligible, but I agree he must be the youngest guest among us. Maybe he has the kind of cancer that doesn't announce itself, but he does look ok to me. Maybe he was disappointed in love and he's here for us ladies."

"You are such a scandal, Susy girl! Never thought of that. We'll have to keep our doors locked at night."

"You should be so lucky. You know the Doctor never much mixed since he's been here. And he never has family visits. Maybe they knew each other before."

"I was listening to the birds the other day on the porch. Jason the boy from the kitchen wheeled me out. I must have nodded off. When I awoke, they were together on the davenport, swinging and swaying. I heard the Yankee say something like, 'There are always stories that need to be told.'"

"We all have our stories, Bea. As you know I'd rather forget mine."

"Well I think the fellow came here to be with the Doctor. I saw him the first day. He looked for him in the dining room. I'll bet he needs something from the great medical man."

"Oh, you are into one of your made-up stories. Next, you'll be telling me he's an alien who was sent from another planet to learn about a secret cure."

"Now you are exaggerating, Susy. I'm just a silly woman and I don't know what it is but I'm telling you my in-too-ishon says he wants something from the Doctor and he is going to get it before the old man leaves us."

The Story of My Life

"The things I've seen."

"I'll bet, Doctor, I'll bet." North answered.

"You will really help me with a memoir? You think it's the right thing to do?"

"It has to do with truth. I think we should all clear the ledger before we go, especially if there is a something that should come out that hasn't. For myself, I have some secrets that might shock people; I'm going to find a way to tell some uncomfortable truths. In your case it sounds to me that you have hinted there are some things to say that people need to hear but I really don't think you should bother unless you go right at it. You know we'll both be gone soon. And forgotten. But a book lives on."

"I think your people, not that I underestimate you, but because you seem different... I think that your people are probably typical Yankee believers in the federal government. The federals don't understand the South. And they've wronged us again and again. But I'm slowing down. I keep grasping for words. Your name for example. You've told me but I can't bring it back."

"My name is Christopher North."

"That's right, I remember now, but it is funny. Unusual isn't it that you have a sort of Yankee name but you said you'd help me. North helps South. Gotta laugh, right?"

"Right."

"I was once the most important man in Gulf City. You may think I'm making that up but I'm not bragging. The Medical Center. 'The Tower,' they call it. My doing. When the politicians got sick guess who they called?"

"You told me this before but when I ask for the full story you always describe your best surgeries. Is that what you mean by being the most important? Were you a renegade or rebel bucking the system?"

They were on the lakeside path. Ronson stopped his slow walk and turned toward North.

"Only a Yankee would think that. I was the protector of the hospital from the federals. The staff doctors were a bunch of snivelers. I had to take care of them. They wanted this, they wanted that. But when it came to action, to the doing, they put hands over their ears and... Oh, I can't remember. Having trouble with my words. It starts with an 's.'"

"Well, what are you trying to say?"

"They put this thing over their ears so they wouldn't hear. I had to do everything."

"What kind of thing?"

"Huh."

"Over their eyes?"

"No, over their ears. It's what you use to tell about the heart."

"Stethoscopes?"

"That's it. It was like they put on their stethoscopes. What was I saying?"

"That your fellow docs were avoiding something and you had to take care of it. Did you say it was a person?"

"Right. Sounds right. I built a great medical center. Someone was in the way. I need to go back now. I'm feeling ... perhaps it's just bradykinesia."

"What is that? 'Bradykinesia' or some word like that is what I think you said."

"Did I? Yes, I did. I must have. 'Bradykinesia' just means I'm getting to be a very slow walker. I do think we need to go back. A bit dizzy. You are a true friend."

North made sure Ronson returned safely to his room. He left the main building and found his car in the far parking lot. He turned on the engine to charge the battery. Sat behind the wheel and remembered his last conversations with Orzell Williams. "I know what you're thinking," he said, "but you have to let her go. You can't bring her back by searching for more of the story. Look forward, not back. You should follow the teachings of your religion."

"My religion? Orzell, I think believing in religion it is pretty much like believing in justice. It's important that people think it's possible to attain even if they are buying a myth."

"Now, now. Look, we were both brought up in religions where God was less important than that we were at one with the other worshipers—right?"

"You got me all wrong. My father, Finian, was Irish Catholic but not one who would be caught practicing. He didn't talk much about it but turned out he hated the priests and nuns who had taught him in school. My mother, well, she was brought up by Jewish socialists who disdained God-talk; she wasn't interested in their way or in the ways they rejected. I think both parents liked that they could pretend they didn't do religion because of who they married, but it was just an excuse. They just had no feeling for it. It didn't enter into their thinking."

"Hard to believe. For me the music, the singing, and the listening to it, is unforgettable. That's where the feeling comes in but it stops there. No notion about God with me. It's a social thing. But it's a stupid political thing to dis it. You just don't dis it."

"If you do the law, Orzell, you don't have to be religious. You don't have to believe."

"By your lights, what is the law?"

"Playing by the old rules in the old book, I guess. I have a college classmate. Very observant. Sincere. Hard on secular types like me. But never in my hearing has he mentioned God."

"To play by the rules do you have to go to synagogue like I have to go to church?"

"Something like that. Observe all the rituals and you're all right. It's like the coin toss on the field before a football game. Who gets the ball first if a team wants it. The matter has been decided before the teams step onto the field—but you have to go through the public coin toss anyway."

"Before?"

"Before means as written down in the books and scrolls. The tradition. What the really old guys have set down."

"And there is no ... deviation?"

"Orzell, where Jews are concerned there is always deviation. They are—or should I say *we are*? I never know... A contentious people. You probably have never heard the line—two Jews, three political parties."

"Always an education, Christopher. Ah, your name. As I have said, very strange, a Jew named after The Savior."

The Pistol

Before coming to Comfort Acres, North had attended three Alabama gun shows. He browsed the firearms and accessories, ammunition, even knives and the clothing sold for hunters. He paused at a table with membership brochures from the National Rifle Association and at another with handouts promoting Second Amendment rights. He was told by a pamphlet he picked up at the door that the reason he was at a show called a "loophole," one that allowed him to buy without questions or identity checks, was nothing but a derogatory reference; that certain "liberal" groups had invented the bad-sounding label for what was legal conduct.

He was careful not to talk to any of the sellers directly but stood behind prospective buyers listening to their questions, took a few notes of the makes available, and paused before tables holding antique firearms, ammunition and cowboy pistols of which he had no interest. He saw what he wanted early, a used Browning Hi-Power 9mm pistol designed years earlier by an American but originally Belgian made. He knew the gun well from its appearance in one of his old prosecution cases. It had been acquired by both sides during World War II. The Germans used it when they captured Belgium production facilities but design plans were eventually smuggled out of Belgium and wound up in the hands of a Canadian gun manufacturer; suddenly it was the weapon carried by British fliers, U.S. allies and agents of the Office of Strategic Services, the precursor to the CIA. The Browning had a magazine capacity of ten rounds; lethal at fifty-five yards and easy to disassemble and reassemble. The pistol was compact and light. He could have bought the gun in two of the three Alabama shows but drove three hours across the state to the annual show held at small Mississippi town rumored to be casual in its recordkeeping. Most important for North, it was the make of the weapon that killed Clem.

A week before the final move to Comfort Acres, North drove to an Eastside Gulf City auto parts supply store. With cash, he purchased a magnetic steel box. On a busy Saturday, he drove across town to a Goodyear Tire Store near a sprawling suburban mall and bought four new whitewalls. While the aging Chevrolet was on the lift, he watched the mechanic balancing the tires. He pulled out a ten-dollar bill, thanked the man for what he was doing, and then asked him to get him a glass of water so he could take a pill. While the mechanic was gone, North slipped the box under the chassis near the muffler assembly. Later, he parked the car in a far corner of The Acres parking lot among the vehicles of long-time residents. Many guests rarely drove but they still kept their cars.

After breakfast each day, North and Ronson took their lakeside walk. At first, the talk was mostly about Comfort Acres itself, its policies and residents. North found that the doctor liked to make fun, even ridicule, of those around him. Neither the staff nor fellow residents were immune. North would gently laugh as the doctor brought out their foibles as he saw them, keeping his eyes on the path, even putting his arm around the older man to steer him over an uneven slab of paving or a protruding root where the concrete ended. North did a lot of nodding but spoke little. It didn't matter.

Ronson mostly talked as if to himself. But, after a month in which they saw each other almost every day, a month in which North grew frustrated, not so much with the slow pace of their relationship but with his own indecision. Hours spent alone in his room, he did some legal work requested by old friends and colleagues; mostly turning out background briefing material in criminal cases that asked the courts to take a more vigorous role in protecting defendant's rights.

But his sense of a society progressing toward justice had ebbed. He expected his arguments would fall on deaf ears but had decided long ago that they still had to be pursued. North began to feel like a man who was too familiar with lost causes and he tried to comfort himself by reading the fattest books he could find. But he failed to finish all of Joyce's *Ulysses*; couldn't get past the first few chapters of *Finnegan's Wake*. Finally, he found an interest in the Hebrew Bible, though it tended to bring on a nap.

Six weeks in, he began to make progress. Ronson was beginning to talk of his life as a surgeon, spinning off tales of lives saved, especially of breasts removed. He told of misdiagnoses by colleagues, usually a story that had him riding to the rescue. North was bored but he affected interest. He was beginning to feel he had Ronson's confidence but knew the connection had to deepen.

He'd stoke the growing dependency by absence. He told Ronson he would be going on a visit to his son who was a lawyer in Boston. At the news, the doctor looked lost. He told North again and again that he was dancing with Parkinson's. He was delicate. He hoped his trip would be short.

Over the weeks, Ronson's symptoms had grown more troublesome. He was walking slower, and trembling more; occasionally on their walks he would take hold of North to avoid falling. "You are a true friend," the doctor kept saying, "a true friend." As he held on to a shoulder, he told North he was a master diagnostician. He knew he was losing brain cells. Being a doctor means you can map your own decline. But then for a time he would seem to have a settled back into an almost normal phase. North watched and waited. He would have to find a medical book.

North had the Browning in his car but brushed aside the thought. He told himself it would have to wait. He did not like violence. *But could revenge make a difference?* Unlike capital punishment, there were no passing-the-buck officials refusing to take responsibility for the killing. No cant about closure for victims' families or politicians playing the tough-on-crime game. He tried to see revenge as something else. It was personal, and hadn't he changed his life so it would include the personal? He told himself you could think someone deserved to die and still be against extreme punishment from bureaucratic institutions that promoted a dysfunctional system, one that killed poor men, or those of the wrong race, or even the innocent, with lousy lawyers.

Did he really believe he could kill the man? North certainly wanted him dead but the lawyer in him shouted a different message. *Find a better way to get what you want.* That he couldn't settle on how to do it made him aware that he hadn't yet decided he could do it.

Before North left for Boston, he'd put the memoir idea to Ronson again, not at all sure that the doctor could hold the thought in his mind. Still, it would be a start: "You know you had a great career. Cutting-edge medicine as I understand it, and you haven't even commented on your years running that state-of-the-art hospital. You and I are getting near the end; I'm thinking about telling my story. You should do the same. While I'm gone I'm going to talk to a professor who helps people remember. I'll let you know what she says."

And then North was off, leaving Ronson stonefaced. Hands betraying the characteristic shakes. North wasn't sure he would be able to hold on to the conversation but the seed had been planted.

Research

North stood and waited, feeling utterly lost at the reference desk of the Countway Library of Medicine in the hospital district of Boston. He'd been told that this was the place to go, but felt out of his element. The library served the Harvard Medical School and everyone he passed in the halls looked like a serious professional on an important medical mission. The librarian, a middle-aged, gray-haired woman, had a welcoming smile, but she made him repeat his request three times before she understood that he was interested in the symptoms associated with Parkinson's Disease, symptoms other than the usual slowness of movement, stiffness, tremors, difficulty of walking, and the like. North apologized that he was not being particularly clear.

"You want to know what other conditions Parkinson's is associated with is that correct?"

"Correct."

"And you aren't a physician?" she inquired.

"No just a friend of one who is suffering," North replied.

"Well, come with me then and we'll try to find a tome that isn't too full of jargon and medical Latin."

"That would be helpful."

"But I am curious," she added, "tell me, what do you expect to do for this friend of yours?"

"I'm not sure."

"And you say he—and it is a he, I understand—is a doctor?"

"Yes, that is true."

"Well I need to caution you, sir, to be careful telling a doctor, even one suffering, what to do."

North felt he was about to explode. It was the old North that came back. He saw this seemingly pleasant woman as a pure intrusion, a meddler, a micromanager. Just because he wasn't wearing a white lab coat. Anger rode over him like a towering ocean wave and then just as suddenly it disappeared. The wave hit the shore and was gone. Not only was she doing her job. Not only was his inner roar coming from what he recognized as an ancient place of ambivalence about female authority, but given his intentions she was, of course, doing him an enormous favor. He must be on edge because he didn't like what he was doing and yet couldn't stop doing it.

"I thank you for that," he offered in the most soothing voice he could muster. "I'm just researching this for my friend. He can't any longer do it for himself and," here he paused, "it's what he deserves."

She led him to a smooth-grained oak library table and seated him at a corner under a bright overhead light. After excusing herself, some minutes later she pushed a cart with three thick medical books to his side. She took a seat next to him. She opened the books to various chapters, bookmarking selections with plastic cards. Pointing to the cards, she told him the information he wanted would be summarized at those excerpts. "When you are finished," she added, "replace the books on the cart. Staff will reshelve them." She wished him good luck and left.

As he sat at the table confronting the three medical books, North opened a brief case, extracted a yellow legal pad and began to take notes.

Parkinson's is associated with Dementia. Lewy Bodies (DLB) for progressive dementia has similar symptoms.

DLB and Alzheimer's also have similar symptoms. How about pneumonia—Aspiration? Bacterial?

Aspiration—food, stomach acid in lungs? Maybe. Renal Failure related to BHP. Bacterial infection—fluid, pus, debris in cells lowered immunity/treat with antibiotics but problematic.

Look for mucus—green, yellow? Coughing, fever.

After an hour, head spinning, North found what he was looking for. He closed the books. Placed them on the cart, folding the sheets with his notes in half and then in half again and placing them in his briefcase. He left the library and headed for the airport. Halfway there, he dismissed the cab. Walked until he came to a pharmacy. He searched the vitamin aisle, at first without success. Then he dropped to his knees; on a bottom shelf he found a bottle labeled "Lo-Salt."

The Professor

L ater that day, North was in Philadelphia. The professor was anxious to see him but annoyed that it had taken so long to happen; not that she fully trusted the man who had called, referred by Olivia Martine, even though he said he was the man who she had wanted to talk to. He was a lawyer, of course, which was fine. Despite the reputation of some, she actually liked lawyers. They were serious about their work and so was she. They believed in evidence and so did she. He said he was responding to her information about the death of Doctor Clem and that was what she wanted to hear, but still it was months, even years, too late. Of course, she'd see him. What else could she do? She knew in her gut that she wanted the death pursued. But little was likely to come of it.

These cold case people, and she assumed he was like them, were intense and relentless in their research. And so was she, but really, what had it accomplished? True, the cold case people had excavated dozens of murders. Brought out stories for all to see of police shootings of Black men that the local press had never pursued, of grand juries declining to indict clear cases of homicide. She knew from their findings that, even in the very few cases that went to all-white trial juries, they decided to acquit. The families of the victims loved the cold case research warriors. They had lived with half stories, myths, lack of documentation and even lies. And suddenly, the faculty researchers and their enthusiastic students appeared with death certificates and coroner's reports they hadn't imagined existed, musty court records that had never been shared, letters from the NAACP to law enforcement, FBI reports. Every once in a while, they actually moved government to do something, but rare as a successful prosecution was, the families relished learning and being a center of attention. Sometimes memorials were created; a few sheriffs had even apologized for what had happened in their jurisdiction years before. Of course, this usually happened where the racial composition of the voter list had radically changed.

She thought all this was worthwhile, but in truth that wasn't her concern with the case of Doctor Clem. She was not family. Her interest in the civil rights movement was longstanding; after all, she taught American history. But she had to admit that she still cared because once she had cared a lot. It had been her tenure piece. The article that sealed the deal with the faculty, then almost all males, that she was a real scholar. The work on medical care and discrimination. The story of how the feds actually turned the tables on hundreds of hospitals that excluded Blacks or kept them in separate second-class wards, refused to allow their doctors in, treated their nurses like cleaners. The countless deaths that followed.

The facts were not really unknown but no one had documented them as she had. No one had visited, as she had, forty-seven of these medical facilities in six states; no one else had interviewed dozens of the civil servants who had streamed South in the sixties to inspect the hospitals and somehow persuaded most of them to comply with the civil rights laws. She had the numbers. She had more footnotes than she needed. And her work erased any doubts that she deserved tenure.

Afterwards, after all these years, she thrived. But had never forgotten what happened to the Doctor Clem. How any real investigation had been shunted aside. She always believed it was a murder and she had a strong suspicion as to what happened. The Gulf City reaction left her with nothing but doubt. She could never forgive or forget the way Clem, who she had interviewed early on, who she had a drink with in a Gulf City hotel bar months before her death, was tarred after she couldn't respond. Called a drug addict, a secret lover of a Black man, and an aggressive lesbian. A trifecta all right. But it was the last claim—the dyke claim—that stuck with her. And made it a personal matter. She took it very personally, *as if it would be ok to kill Clem because of it.*

The professor wanted to see the lawyer even though there was no way to know where it would go.

When he came to her office it was a shock. He didn't hold back. He told her he worked on good guy cases of all sorts from an office in Gulf City. That he and Clem had been lovers. He knew she was a mole. In fact, he had set it up with a key player in Washington. He felt responsible for her death though he believed Clem had been unmasked by a foolish phone call, adding a few details she had never been sure of. He rattled all this out quickly. It was like, she thought, he had to dump it somewhere, get it off his chest maybe or more likely, she decided, to stop obsessing. To loosen the ties of obvious depression.

Then he stopped. Sipped the chamomile tea she had offered. Was he waiting for her or did he have more to say? They were silent as if expecting a visitor who would come and tell them what to do.

Finally, he came out with it: "I am almost certain I know who was responsible but it will put me more at ease if you can confirm it, even if it's just your informed guess."

When he told her, she did a slow, deep nod. Then she asked how he found out.

He shook his head. "I can't tell you the specifics but it followed from a source in law enforcement. The tip led to a criminal who talked. I'm curious, more than curious—how did you find out what you know about the killing?"

"Remember," she answered, "I'm a professional researcher. A kind of high-class snoop. It was mostly circumstantial. I spent a week in Gulf City talking to everyone, though I have to accept that I failed to find you. It was clear to me that the whole thing was cooked, but I was frustrated that I couldn't put a name or face to it. Early on, I got an interview with Hedley Ronson. It was a short time after Clem was found dead. I had been there to research the whole business of how hospitals dealt with racial change. He didn't know I knew Clem and had talked to her earlier as a background source. He certainly didn't know she felt that she was at risk. He told me about the tower, about his plans for making Davis Memorial into a powerhouse. He insisted his medical staff would act in a totally equitable and nondiscriminatory manner as long as they could exercise independent judgment over how their patients were treated. It was all very cordial; that's the only way I know to interview. Otherwise you can drift into hostility and then you get nothing of value.

"Then something unexpected happened. I asked him for the hospital's written policy on race and what papers it had submitted to the federal government. He said of course I could have the complete record. He asked his secretary to put together a file. As she was leaving, he asked her to call someone for him. I sat by her desk just outside his office while she went off to get what I had asked for. The door to his office was open just a crack but it was enough to hear he was telling someone about the Clem's death. There was triumph in his voice. The only words I heard were something like, 'Just thought you people should know. You better keep your people safe.' From what he said, but more from the way he said it, then I knew in my heart that he was involved. I didn't know how. But later when I learned he was talking to the Washington regulators, the people who had vexed him. Well then, I decided, I was right."

North could hardly contain himself. He stood and walked to her office window, staring out at a quad where students were tossing a Frisbee.

"Professor, what would you do now if you had enough facts to be sure?"

"I guess I'd report him to the authorities. There's no statute of limitations for murder is there?"

"No there isn't, but that a case can be brought doesn't mean a case will be brought. In the City where I work, a prosecution is a nonstarter."

"Would an exposé in the press serve any purpose? Olivia would know how to get the story out."

"It would become known, but I'm not sure he'd even learn about it. He has a series of medical complaints marching toward dementia."

"Oh my," she said, "I guess you'll just have to bump him off."

"Precisely. And thanks, also, for the tea." North made to leave.

"Whoa, now, you're welcome but promise me if you establish what we both think, if you become absolutely sure he did it, you'll let me know." She suddenly started to sneeze. "Give me a minute. I need a tissue; must be allergy season. Please sit down. I believe you're serious."

North said nothing but the professor went on in between sneezes. "Listen I'm older than you are and I'm not your mother but do consider where you are coming from. I would like him dead, too, but for me it's just an idea. I don't have a guilty conscience. I couldn't have saved her. I don't have any guilt. Just anger. But you say you arranged her relationship with the federal inspectors." Her sneezing became convulsive.

The professor bent over to reach down to the bottom drawer in her desk, searching for a box of tissues. When she raised her head, North was gone.

Georgia

She had never been given the title of "general manager" that she deserved by the corporate owners in Dallas, much less the salary. Still she was in charge of day-to-day arrangements and liked to exercise her authority. Georgia was convinced The Acres would fall apart if she released her grip. *The* guests were *her* guests. On her daily rounds, she approached the two ladies in wheelchairs.

"Susie, here comes Miss Georgia and I'm going to ask her opinion."

"Opinion of what?"

"Of the Yankee and the Doctor of course.

"Bea, you are beginning to sound like a ridiculous old lady but don't let me stop you. I'm curious too."

"Hello, Miss Georgia, we want to compliment you on the weekend buffet. So much improved."

"We do our best ladies. And we treasure your suggestions."

"We had a question."

"Of course."

"We think it so very nice that our young man, the Yankee, takes such good care of Doctor Ronson. They are quite a pair."

"Do you have a question Beatrice?"

"Do you think his attentions are a shade unusual? And he seems so young to be here. And his talk. He isn't from here of course."

"Ladies, as you know, I make it a practice not to gossip. The privacy of all our residents is very important. But you two are among our most esteemed guests and I have to admit I share some of your interest in the subject. I will tell you that the cleaners report Mr. North's room is a mess of books and legal looking documents. He seems to be very active for a man who is supposed to be retired. I am assured that this information will not be shared with others."

"What do you think about him and the doctor?"

"Yes, I agree. Inseparable. When Mr. North was absent on a trip, the doctor lost some ground. He got angry at his waiter, Conrad. Such a gentle soul. He told him the soup was cold and Conrad, of course, brought him another portion the kitchen had heated up but he rejected the new bowl too. And he said, 'Why are you bringing me this?' The doctor seems to have lost his appetite. Conrad told us he was even afraid the he was going to throw the hot soup bowl at him."

"Do you trust Mr. North?"

"Why, Susie, what a question! Do you have any reason we should be concerned?"

"I don't know. I don't know. But these Yankees. They don't belong here. And a lawyer. They are usually people with motives."

"What do you think, Beatrice?"

"I never like to think ill. He seems to care. Actually, he does look more like a caretaker than one of our fellow guests and I agree the doctor is not doing well. I've heard he bribed one of the colored attendants for extra ice cream brought to his room the other night but usually he eats like a sparrow."

"And you agree, Susie, right?"

"Bea and I think alike. I don't like to gossip either but it's well known that on nights when, of course, you are back at your home, he wanders the hallways. Sometimes he walks like a man in pain. If anyone has left things downstairs in the lounge he'll take them to his room. They have often been discreetly returned."

"Yes. I've heard some of this. But the doctor is an honored guest. All of you are, of course. Still, we know what an important person he was in the community, what with Davis Memorial and all. But talking to you dears, I think I should be paying more attention. All guests are *my* guests. We have our ways of keeping track. I'll look into it. You know, completely between us, we have consultant for things like this. A Gulf City man who spent his career doing detective work. I'll talk to him. We definitely need a visit."

The Science of Death

It took North the better part of a morning to convert the medical jargon into plain English. He wondered how most doctors seemed to throw Latinate terms around as if they were born to them. Was it more than a way of keeping the common people at bay? He did his best to translate what he read into English:

The use of potassium salts is contraindicated in patients with an enlarged prostate because it can obstruct the flow of urine, and this in turn can contribute severe renal impairment. Renal failure may occur when the kidneys can no longer remove waste from the bloodstream. Since potassium is excreted by the kidney, the administration of potassium salts in such patients, may produce hyperkalemia—an abnormally high potassium level—and cardiac arrhythmias or arrest.

The product he found over the counter in a Boston pharmacy called "Lo-Salt" contained at least two thirds potassium chloride but it looked just like the table salt you could buy at your local supermarket. North wondered how many deaths in hospitals had occurred as a result of mistaken introduction of this salt substitute to patients with what the docs called BHP—an enlarged prostate—who also had serious kidney issues.

Then, browsing through a legal newspaper with a national focus published in Washington, he learned, to his astonishment, that the potassium chloride salt substitute he'd acquired was the drug that caused death in the executions under a lethal injection protocol just then employed for executions in the state of Oklahoma. It was thought that if the drug worked to the satisfaction of prison officials, lethal injections might replace electric chairs and gas chambers nationally as a means of execution. Though the other two drugs used in Oklahoma were administered in lethal dosages and would, in time, produce the prisoner's death, the same potassium chloride he'd bought over the counter in a drug store was being employed to bring about cardiac arrest and death within a minute of injection. To check his facts, North found a drug handbook in the Gulf City central library and read that, while potassium chloride acts quickly, it is excruciatingly painful if administered without proper anesthesia.

North sat for a long time at the library desk with the open book in front of him. The air conditioning was powerful but it regularly made a heaving sound that sent stronger currents of air through the room. With only a light shirt, North shivered and felt chilled. But he also felt unable to move. The thought finally formed in the chaos of his mind: if the Lo-Salt worked on the kidneys as expected, it would amount to minutes of torture. If he bungled the process, Ronson's suffering would be worse. He banged his fist on the table. Heads turned at the noise. He realized he would have to find another way. While North admired both the wrongly convicted and the funeral orators who could urge forgiveness, he did not believe in forgiveness and redemption. Change, yes, but forgiveness and redemption that had a cosmic, religious, feel? No, it just wasn't him. But if he could not kill or let it pass, what then? Was he just a silent bystander to an evil? An evil that had torn the pages of his life?

He closed the book, thanked a helpful librarian on the way out, and lost himself walking the city for the next five hours.

Elder Abuse

"So, again, you've told me you have a lot of stories to tell. That you were the man who put Gulf City on the medical map."

Ronson talked more slowly than he had before North had left on his trip to Boston and Philadelphia. It was an obvious effort to get the word out. "There is some truth to that, but should I brag?"

"Why not?"

"It was all because those sons of bitches. Those sons of bitches on the surgery staff thought I should stop operating even though I was their chief of surgery. Unheard of. Sons of bitches!"

"But you showed 'em."

"Yeah I showed 'em." Ronson paused. "And the federals too."

"How do the federal government get involved in this?"

"Turn on that recorder you have to make a memoir. I want everyone to know this. The Democrats in the government wanted to take away our right to place patients where it was best for them. They did it for race. They did it for Negro voters. They were, what is the word, *race, race, race...*"

"–ist?"

"What?"

181

"Racist."

"That's right, they were the real racists."

"The federal government was racist?"

"Yes, we loved our colored patients and wanted the best for them—but these race mixers wanted us to do it their way. We wouldn't have it. The colored, they really preferred their own facility."

"By then you were in charge?"

"I told them I would never give in. I had the Governor on my side. We had a strategy. Knew what we were doing."

"And how did you fight?"

"I bet you'd like to know. I think that must be privileged. Everyone would like to know. They sent a joker from Washington to get tough with us but we took care of him all right. If I could get my hands on him now I'd shake him plenty. But after, something happened, the federals caved. They decided they couldn't beat us. So we built the tower. The medical tower. All glass. Could see it thirty miles away. Latest machines. How do you say it, state-of-the-art? You should see the hyperbaric chamber. The best in the region. It has been compared to Boston. What was I talking about?"

"Oh, forget it. You're angry. Tell me about your family?"

"You're so good to be interested. You care but the hospital doesn't. They gave me a plaque but they've forgotten all I've done. I don't exist for them anymore. I thought they'd name the new building annex after me but they've forgotten me. But I really don't mind."

"Your family?"

"I have a daughter. She is in, I think, California. Maybe the movie business. She sends me a basket of fruit. She'll come to visit one day I'm sure, but she is so busy."

"And a wife?"

"That's an old story. My childhood sweetheart. But we parted. Not compatible is what we were. My work was too important. The truth is can't even remember her name. Imagine that. I'm losing it."

"Let's stop for today. Should I turn the machine off?"

"You are a true friend and so patient with me."

"I just love stories and most of all stories of men who took a stand. Who did the hard thing to get results. I'll bet we could make a book out of your life. A man who changed lives. Maybe even a movie. Did you do anything you regret?"

"Of course. You can't build hospital towers when the people around you don't understand without…"

"Without?"

"Taking action."

"And do you want to tell me what action?"

"I'm not sure. Maybe tomorrow."

The Deal

North thought he'd give it a few more days but he was aware that the desire for revenge had turned inward. He felt limp. He was beginning to doubt and punish himself. But Ronson wanted to talk. "You know," he said again, "one of the things you get along with an MD is you can diagnose yourself. I have that skill. I can watch my own dying. I can see what is happening to me and I have decided that I need your help."

"Whoa, I'm not sure where you're going."

"Christopher, its ok I call you that, isn't it?" He spoke slowly, dragging the words out. "We haven't always been using names. I don't have any family members nearby and even if they were nearby I wouldn't trust them. My older brother Benson. He's always out for himself. We haven't spoken in some time. He's off in Florida somewhere with his third wife."

"Your daughter?"

"She is far away and not what I need. She has gone over to Hollywood-type thinking."

"And what you need is?"

"Someone who will see that I get to leave on my own terms. Don't pretend you don't know what I mean. Now, when I still have some mind left, or at least hope I do, I have to arrange things. See things right. I'm not always sure where I am going or what I am doing. I've lost my appetite. The food is so tasteless; I have to smother it with salt to get it down. A regular pee is a sometimes thing. The other day I had this urge to throw a soup bowl at someone. I'm not sure whether I did or not but I know I wanted to."

"Hedley, are you sure you trust me to do what has to be done? What about the staff here?"

"They are part of the problem. I don't trust them either. I'll be put on some damn machine. Tubes will be inserted that will never come out. I believe you only have my best interests at heart. You aren't from around here. I'm thinking you don't have any mixed loyalties."

"Oh, I have my own needs. Don't be misled about that. I usually do the things I want to do, one way or another. But tell me specifics."

"I need to work them out. I haven't been paying attention to what drugs I might need. I'm not even sure I'm still authorized to write a prescription. You need to keep up on registration with the state for that. There are other options. I can always shoot myself."

"Would you really want to do that?"

"Well, I'm not scared of it if it's necessary. We grow up with firearms around here. One bang in the right place and everything is all over. 'Sayonara,' as they say. But I don't have a gun right now. That's the sort of thing I need help with. I doubt I'd be in shape to press the trigger. I'd ask you to do it but then you'd get in trouble. We don't have the right laws around here." Ronson tried to raise himself from the bed but failed and fell back. North could have intervened but he didn't move. "I'll tell you a secret, Christopher."

"Yes."

But suddenly, Ronson was silent.

"Yes, you were saying Hedley?"

"I'm not sure."

"Something about a secret."

"A secret? Yes, I think I was saying I don't know a doctor who hasn't put someone out of their misery at the end. We all deny it. The Catholics most of all. But we all do it. Anyway, guns are messy. Someone would have to clean up the blood. There is also the plastic bag way. I know of a case like that but it takes too long. Not sure I can hold my breath if that's required."

"I know the case," North replied. "It was reported in the papers. The woman was first made very drowsy with sleeping pills but she then tried to pull off the bag. It left her with a horrible death."

"I knew you'd be the right person. You have ideas. Experience, I'll bet."

"But aren't we a long way from this sort of thing?"

"What I've got builds over the years. For me it comes in waves and one day soon the waves will knock me over and I won't get up. Maybe I could get someone to find me some morphine. That's what we have used on terminal patients. You know, I'll pay you to do it. I have plenty of money that I can't take with me."

"Forget about that. I don't want money. I want us to finish your life story. Especially how you were able to turn this sleepy hospital into a regional power, even a national success story. How you out-foxed the federals; even got them to kick in the financing. That's my interest."

"Yes, it's a big story. Very important. But you're the only one who cares about it. If I went back to Davis Memorial tomorrow I wouldn't know hardly anybody. You can bet they wouldn't recognize me. Why are you so interested?"

"Maybe we'll find out when you tell the story."

Coming Clean

Northdecided he'd give it one more day. They were in Ronson's room. A tray with food was untouched.

"You were gone," Ronson said.

"Yes, you knew that. I've been back a while."

"Was it a longtime? Felt like it."

"I'm flattered you missed me."

"No one to talk to here. Not sure why I'm in this place."

"You've told me you needed to be near people who would take care of you. Why not your former colleagues?"

"They've moved on. I'm not in touch. But if you're sick here and you need help you get someone schooled on a Caribbean Island. And, of course, they speak funny. They clean my room and the food is barely edible, don't you think?"

"You get what you pay for."

"So, you went somewhere ... you told me, but..."

"I checked in on a colleague in Philadelphia. I also saw a man in prison here for murder. I had to talk to him about a legal matter. Should we continue talking about your life story?"

"Where were we?"

"You were telling me how you kept the federal authorities from interfering with your hospital."

"I was? Well, turn on the tape again. I'm proud of this. I kept the Hospital the way it should be, and we got the tower."

"You were proud."

"Where should I start?"

"The man I saw in prison was Osborn Jennings."

"Jennings, Jennings, I knew the family. I'm trying to remember. I'm sending the bucket down the well and when I pull it up sometimes the memories are there. What did he do to be in prison?"

"Arranged to have a woman killed."

"What kind of a woman?"

"His wife."

"Did she deserve it?"

"What could she do to deserve it?"

"Some women don't do good things."

"You mean betrayals?"

"Yes, that's what I mean, betrayals."

"Has a woman ever betrayed you?"

"Is the recording machine on?"

"Yes. Do you want me to turn it off?"

"No, keep it on."

"You want it on?"

"Yes."

"Done. Now what do you want to say?"

"Jennings comes from a family of scoundrels. They're Sheet people. He was a troublemaker. He was supposed to scare her. Make her shut up."

"He did something wrong?"

"Terrible."

"And you were in charge of the hospital?"

"I always did what was best for my people. We had to have the new building. The grant."

"That's why you were the boss."

"No one else would do anything to protect our way of life."

"What would you say if Jennings told me you ordered it?"

"I'd say she was supposed to be put on notice."

"Are you feeling ok right now? Why do you still want the tape running?"

"Of course, there should be a record of how I saved the situation. You know our people always lost wars but we always won the peace."

"What if Jennings makes a fuss with the authorities? Men in his position will say anything to escape execution."

"They would recognize how important the hospital was to community wellbeing. People down here don't take crap from the race mixers."

"You mean white people wouldn't?"

"No, no I'm not prejudiced. Doctors have to be in charge. Not those fools in Washington. We also found ways to take care of the colored people; everything that I did was done to preserve medicine for those who know what to do with it."

"What I hear is an absence of guilt."

"Guilt for what?"

"That's what I mean. I think we are done for today. You need your rest and so do I. But a last question: what do you want me to do with the tape? Do you want me to destroy it?"

"What an idea! I heard a while back that there's a new University coming to Gulf City, a branch of the State U. They'll keep history records, won't they? Get them to set up an archive. Put my name on it. Place it there so students in the future will know my devotion."

A Phone Call

North drove a few miles from The Acres, down a strip road of gas stations, fast food places, and chain motels to the nearest post office. The man behind the counter wore a vest with various fishing lures pinned to the fabric. For a moment, North found it hard to take his eyes off the array of yellow and orange plastic feathers covering the man's chest. He bought a book of stamps he didn't need, then begged a few dollars in quarters. When they were reluctantly handed over, he retreated to a phone booth on the side of the building.

He wasn't happy making the call but he'd promised the professor a report of what he found. She had begun the process with her research and deserved to know, or so he told himself. When he said that he'd confirmed to his satisfaction that Ronson was behind what Jennings had done, her response was immediate. "Now we can take it to the FBI."

North was irritated by her naïveté. He wanted to think that a rational explanation would set her straight. "We don't have the kind of proof that would be accepted by a prosecutor, much less a court. A sick old man's confession rendered in a kind of code to someone who was conning him, someone he thought was a loyal friend. A murderer facing execution who expects to escape the electric chair if he tells his story. It's the true story, but not the kind that cuts ice in a courtroom. In cases like this, of course, there is never proof of a direct instruction. You know, 'I told him to kill her.' Go see a mob movie, if you don't believe me. The Mafia boss does it all by inference. And..."

She cut him off. "I'm not looking for a judicial process. We'll all be dead by the time that produces anything of value. I just want it out there. Tell it where it will get attention; make it be part of history. Best we can do. This guy thought she was gay. He never would have gone through with it if she was just another waspy Southern Belle, or so I believe. I want this known by the people down there. Up here too. The hell with courts. Don't kill him. Don't indict him. I agree it's a waste of time. Do something else. Do something that works.

"Expose him."

McSorely

McSorely stood next to a pillar on the porch, looking down at the lake. From his vantage he saw what looked to be spreading growth of algae blooms telling him the shallow lake was probably being assaulted by chemicals and sunlight. The future quality of its water and the likelihood of increasing sediment spelled a poor outcome. He wished he had a cigarette but, at his wife's insistence, he had quit. The two men were below him on the shaded part of the path, headed directly to the main house. With his binocs, he could see the one in the wheelchair was gesturing, raising an arm from the armrest and trying to lower it toward his chest as if he was trying to reinforce a point. But it was obvious even for afar that his movement was stiff, tomahawk like. The man pushing the chair had his head bent toward the speaker. But he took a small metal item from a shirt pocket, looked at it as if to check something and returned it to the pocket.

As they came closer, McSorely retreated from the porch to the dining room kitchen. He drew a cup of coffee from a large aluminum urn and made himself comfortable at a table in a corner out of the way of waiters and cooks. He decided there was no need to rush.

The Question

Ronson leaned against a bar in his bathroom while he tried to urinate. After a few dribbles, he called out for help to get to his bed. North steadied him; with outstretched arms moved him into a position where he could be lifted onto the mattress. He straightened the old man's legs and covered the frail body with a light cotton blanket. Ronson's eyes closed. Then opened and fixed on North. Hoarse sounds came from his nose.

North was standing at the end of the bed when the door opened and the former chief of detectives entered the room. He took the gun from a leather bag and offered it to North. "Take it. It's yours. Don't worry it's unloaded." North stared at him. McSorely walked to bedside and said, "Hello, doctor. Nice to see you again." But Ronson did not reply.

McSorely turned back to North. "We all have our firearms in this state but I must say coming across a Browning in a place like this is, to say the least, unusual. Before you object, let me assure you that inspection of your room and vehicle was explicitly authorized by the terms and conditions you signed when you entered The Acres. And let me add that we were careful not to disturb your papers and files."

"Or read them?"

McSorely gave him a crooked smile. "In general, certainly not, though I may have glanced at a few pages while making sure the piles were kept in order and still in the exact place where you left them. What did you intend to do with it?"

"The gun?"

"No, the recorder. I came across an empty box for an Olympus L400 ultra-compact microcassette recorder. Fits in a shirt pocket, they claim. Dictating your memoirs? 'My greatest cases' sort of thing?"

"Perhaps we should step outside if we're going to talk about this."

"I think that's unnecessary."

McSorely went back to the bedside. He leaned in and Ronson rasped, "I know you. Are you here to arrest me?"

"Hard to hear you, sir, but no I'm just in the room to watch what happens to you." Ronson closed his eyes. McSorely turned again to North. "Of course, he isn't dead yet, but while I'm no doctor he isn't long for this world. In Georgia's office, I read his latest medical report from the visiting doc. Pretty grim. Why speed the process with a shooting? You'd just get blood all over the room or maybe bad stuff in his tissues. Law enforcement on the scene, etc."

"You've got it wrong about the gun. I gave up on it long ago, but when he was sentient he talked about suicide by shooting, so I decided to give the Browning to him as a present. But never did it."

"A different method?"

"It's is strange talking calmly with the police about attempted murder. The truth is you provide for someone, get close and assist them, even if not for the right reasons and something changes."

"I'm just here to protect Comfort Acres from embarrassment, that's all. At least that's what they pay me for."

"Still, it is strange."

"Well it looks like the result you want is happening, if not by your hand. He is out of it. What's he got?"

"A laundry list."

"Tell."

"Lewy Body Syndrome. That's a form of dementia. Clumps of protein in the brain where they're not supposed to be. Renal problems. Prostate issues. Hard to pee. Fatigue. Swelling in the ankles, feet, and legs. Shortness of breath."

"Gets us all in the end. What's that bulge in your pants pocket?"

"You are nosey?"

"Hard to give up your work habits even if you've retired."

"Just some salt substitute."

"Hand it over."

North gave it up. He turned to Ronson whose breathing was shallow but the hoarse sounds had stopped.

"Contains potassium chloride. Sounds like something potent. What's it for?"

"We all need potassium. But some don't need too much of it. I'm told too much of it can kill you."

"I think we should let Georgia know she has a guest who may need treatment but we'll let him be for a while."

Ronson tried to raise himself up again but fell back against his pillow. He rasped again.

North ignored him, "He was clear, McSorely, he didn't want heroic methods. No tubes."

"Geez, you're like family, interceding to ensure last wishes and yet, last time we talked you wanted him dead."

"It turns out I'm happy to see him go but not with extreme pain. I'm just a wimp, I suppose."

"Or you've come to your senses. Here's the container of potassium chloride back."

"What should I do with the gun?"

"I'd consider the gift given. Leave it in the bureau drawer. Let Georgia deal with it unless you are listed as the owner, which I doubt. You haven't told me about the recorder yet."

"No, I haven't but you'll find out."

"Aren't we a little late for mysteries?"

"Listen, I'm saying we white liberals are lousy killers. Maybe that's why we lose the big battles. And you're telling me he'll be gone soon. When that happens, I'm an open book. I may be better able to answer your questions then. Today, and for the years after Clem was taken, I've been on autopilot. I'd say I was lost in a moral quagmire but for that you need to know you have no sense of direction. I've been more of a zombie. I've done my cases and gone home at night. The recorder was for the story. For sharing the story. Setting the record straight. Is it enough?

I'll answer my own question: it probably will have to be. But that doesn't leave me satisfied. Let me put it in a way you might understand better. I don't believe in capital punishment. Never have. Told my various bosses never assign me a capital case. Find another prosecutor. Yet without a doubt, I can wish people dead. As you now know, I probably can't take a life but I can at least come close. Might have pulled it off if it weren't for learning of the extreme pain. But remember, I'm an abolitionist. I hate the official way. The way nobody takes responsibility. Somehow the personal still seems ok."

"Ah deep down you're still a macho man," McSorely answered. "Do it yourself like some loner cowboy in the movies seeking revenge. This cop knows all about that. Lived that life, but I'm through with it, and I hope you are too."

North moved close to the man in the bed. "Here's my last question, Hedley. The one I've been waiting to ask until near the end: Ferretti, Sal Ferretti, you had someone listen to his phone call, right? That's how you fingered Clem."

Ronson's breathing labored. He sounded like a runner ending a race. His eyes darted back and forth between his two visitors. "Who's Ferretti?" he finally whispered.

North put his head inches from him and shouted. "The federal man who came. The one you spied on. Fucked over. Then you called Jennings. You know, Ferretti, he killed himself."

Ronson's head slid to his chin. He had stopped hearing.

Cemetery

He had almost finished packing his suitcase when Georgia knocked on his door with a request.

"We'll miss you, Mr. North, but I need your assistance before you go. The arrangements for the doctor are somewhat unsettled; I don't know what to do. I've called the next of kin that we have listed and they haven't been helpful. I thought you being such a friend of the deceased…"

"I think he has a daughter in California."

"I've spoken to her. Well sort of. I mean mostly I listened to a rant. I'm not used to such behavior. Very unsettling."

North snapped closed his bag and waited for her to continue.

"She said or rather screamed at me that she didn't want his money and he should rest in, well, it was rather off-putting. I don't, of course, have anything to do with his estate. She had no interest in deciding where he should be buried or even the, you know, method. I'm being asked by the morticians how the body should be treated."

"There is at least one surviving brother, Georgia. Name is Benson. In Florida, I was told."

"Naturally, I called him next. But he was just as unhelpful. Meanspirited, too, I'd say. He laughed and said 'Just feed him to the fishes.' Those were his exact words. Well I'll never. You know we take a large deposit at entry that can be used at times like this, but I don't know his wishes. I thought you might."

"Is there a will?"

"Not that I know of, but it's not my job to go searching other than what he told us, and he never mentioned anything. What I'm trying to say is *do you have any idea what we should do?* Burial, and if so, where? Or cremation and then what do we do with the ashes? Personally, I find burning an unpleasant concept but as far as we at The Acres know, you are his best and last friend. He hadn't visitors, you know."

"You want my opinion?"

"It would be a blessing."

North sat on his bed and said, "I'm thinking. Have a seat." Georgia took the only chair in the room. She was only a few years from retirement and as she waited she realized problems like this made her yearn for it. The doctor had a temper, she knew, but he was a local celebrity. She didn't expect family members from hell. She looked at North and found a smile slowly forming; his lips retracting in what might be even called a grin.

Noticing her look, North tried appear pensive. Deep into himself he was thinking of the last time he had been close to someone dying. He hadn't gone to Orzell's internment. Marcella hadn't mentioned it at the time, but later, at her request, he'd accompanied her to a stonemason who crafted headstones and monuments. O.W. would be buried at Buena Vista, Gulf City's oldest cemetery. He was buried on a slightly raised piece of land by a glorious magnolia. Somewhat unusual for the South, Marcella told him, even in the slavery era Africans could be buried at Buena Vista though it was thought to be a white cemetery—in the beginning they had to be freemen and women. One area was reserved for confederate soldiers but, after emancipation, plots were sold to anyone who could afford them regardless of who they were. Maybe it was because of the size of the place they want to sell as many plots as they could, she added, so there was no discrimination. She picked out a piece of gray granite with orange striations and handed the mason a note paper on which she'd written the text to be chiseled into the stone: "Orzell Willliams, a man who vanquished evil doers."

The mason frowned. "That's too long. It might fit but better find other words." Marcella was taken aback but she recovered quickly.

"Ok, let's see. Could we just say 'Defeated Evil Doers' instead?" The mason nodded.

Remembering, North almost forgot Georgia's presence but he finally turned to her. "I do have a solution. I know a place in Buena Vista that might be suitable if there's space available. A grave that's just below—actually it will be right at the foot of, right below—a friend of mine. He was a notable citizen of Gulf City. So certainly, it would be more than fitting. I'll take care of the arrangements if it removes a burden from you, but I suspect there will only be room for his ashes. I'll do the headstone too. My gift to a proper remembrance of his life."

"That would be wonderful. I'm so grateful. How would you describe him? On the stone, I mean?"

"Oh, I promise you it will be appropriate. Something that captures what he did in life. Do you have any suggestions?"

"No, I leave it to you. Thanks so much for taking this off my hands. I'm sure it will be a message that speaks to what in life he did."

Payback

Olivia Martine was single-minded. She had always been single-minded. As a child, she remembered all too well, even though it still made her uncomfortable, sassing her mother over almost anything she didn't like.

It took years before she finally accepted that her complaints all emanated from her father being missing. If her mother couldn't hold onto him, Olivia believed, she must be a failure; Olivia would just have to learn to take care of herself. It took even more years for her to gain enough sense to know that her mistakes with men seemed to have their origin in trying to reconstitute the father who had gone missing.

But no one should pity her. She finally got it right in time to find a decent guy and for two late-arriving children, but even before then, it was her work that made the difference. How many Black women could claim the influence she had banked in D.C.? Indeed, few white women either. It had all come from her learning how to work with the details of legislation and federal regulations that few understood; she had learned persistently, quietly and ruthlessly. Not many of the people whose food stamps, rent subsidies, college grants, and disability payments had been preserved or enhanced by her doing would know her name or even recognize her organization, People Defense. She shunned the limelight, but her relations with the press were more than cordial. She knew when a reporter would want to learn that an obscure line in an approved budget would assure a measure protecting those who needed it most. They could keep her name out of it, if that was what she wanted, but they were more than attentive to her wishes.

Olivia was also a prominent call from congressional staffers pondering the intestines of funding legislation so lengthy and complicated that their principals would never read it, and from foundation executives who had to show their liberality and farsightedness by capturing a trend. Olivia was never quite sure how it had all happened. But mulling it over after a second or third glass of wine with her husband, the live-in helper having put the children to bed, she claimed it had to do with a subtle form of guilt manipulation mixed in with a well-known willingness to let others —with the exception of the insiders who depended on her as she depended on them—take the credit.

There was, however, one time a year when she went public, or as she thought of it, quasi-public because she did not overdo promotion. The event was aimed at D.C. scribblers who would look for something previously hidden from view, something that would prove they were not only on the job but able to unearth unknown stories. At the annual Progress Conference, loosely sponsored by the National Press Club, reporters and columnists expected a story with legs would arrive on schedule. After a sumptuous buffet paid for by two large sponsoring law firms, there was a keynote speaker and then a series of breakout panels that would emphasize identifying projects that needed government attention and funding either from the federal budget or private philanthropy. Ample time was allowed for the press to interview speakers and panelists. Olivia would shake every hand worth shaking. Making it a point to embrace, hug, and even kiss in the European style, any man or women who might want her to weigh in on a policy matter or be open to come up with the money needed to support her staff.

When she heard that Chris North was standing at her assistant's desk asking to see her, Olivia told her chief finance officer to excuse her and went to greet him. She saw a North, who, to her eye, amazingly looked younger than when she last saw him at the Acres. North saw a beauty that was thicker but also greater than it had been when more youthful. They stood gaping at each other until Olivia finally broke in and ushered North into her office. "What a surprise," was all she could muster.

"Yes, North replied, very much a surprise." He looked around the room and found what he was after. He removed a cassette recorder and a cable from a shoulder bag. He bent down to attach the cable plug to the outlet. Looking up at Olivia now he spoke a prepared few words.

"You asked me to find the culprit. I appreciated that. I told you that if I did I would kill him. He is dead of natural causes, but he told the story before he died. No doubt you'll want to make the press and the public aware of it at today's conference. Listen up now. Here's the recording. I'm going to press play."

———————————————

Many Thanks

For support and help along the way, many thanks to Alan Childress, Tom Delbanco, Fraser Grier, James Hackney, Elliott Hibbler, Randall Kennedy, Coronna Lain, Daniel Medwed, Rachel Shields, John Siffert, David Smith, Kylie M. Smith, Rose Zoltek-Jick and the support staff of the Northeastern University School of Law. A special shout out for Valerie Ellis of the Mobile Public Library. I couldn't have survived the demands of sixty years as a practicing civil rights lawyer and teacher without the care and concern of more people than I have space to name. Often they educated me without realizing the full measure of their influence but Heli Meltsner has been there since she led me to safely mount a wicked rope ladder hundreds of feet over the boulders of the Nahal Hever. My children Jessica and Molly would be the pride of any parent but I particularly admire their self-possession and integrity. Stan Fisher and the late Harry Subin were true partners in life and law whose laughter and sense of irony an only child needed to grow. Philip Schrag was the academic partner of one's dreams. A lucky man I am to have Evan Mandery as a friend. Thurgood Marshall, Jack Greenberg, and George Cooper gave me the chance to do work I love; Jim Nabrit and Tony Amsterdam taught me how to do it well.

About the Author

Hired by Thurgood Marshall in the 1960s, Michael Meltsner was first assistant counsel to the NAACP Legal Defense Fund during the civil rights era. Among his clients were the doctors and dentists who ended Southern hospital segregation, Muhammad Ali, and numerous death row inmates. He is the author of *The Making of a Civil Rights Lawyer*, the play *In Our Name*, and a celebrated history of the anti-capital punishment movement, *Cruel and Unusual*.

He has taught law at NYU, Columbia, Harvard, and Northeastern— where he is Matthews Distinguished University Professor and the former dean. A recipient of both a Guggenheim and an American Academy of Berlin fellowship, in recognition of his death penalty work, in 2012 he received an honorary doctorate by John Jay College (CUNY). *Mosaic: Who Paid for the Bullet?* is his second novel, after *Short Takes*.

PRAISE FOR *THE MAKING OF A CIVIL RIGHTS LAWYER*

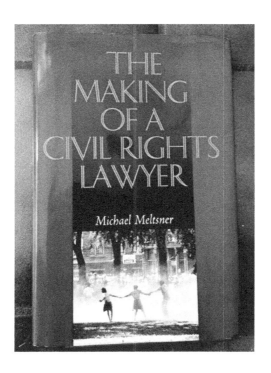

"I once told Michael Meltsner that the story of his life 'the first half devoted to the struggle for civil rights, the second half spent watching in horror as many of those legal victories were overturned' would make a great tragic novel. Unfortunately for me, Meltsner is a novelist, too, and told me he wanted to write it himself. *The Making of a Civil Rights Lawyer* is that book. Not a novel, as it turned out, but peopled with the heroes and villains of that dramatic period in American history."

—Jeffrey Eugenides,
Pulitzer Prize-winning author of *Middlesex*

Visit us at *www.quidprobooks.com.*

Made in the USA
Las Vegas, NV
05 May 2022

48447430R10125